LISTEN TO THIS ISSUE

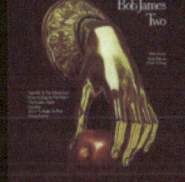

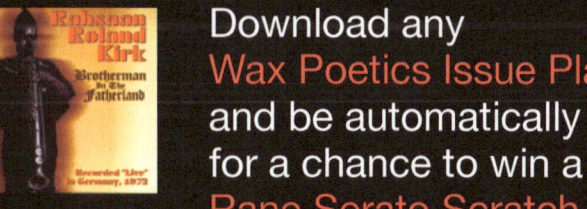

Download any
Wax Poetics Issue Playlist
and be automatically entered
for a chance to win a
Rane Serato Scratch LIVE

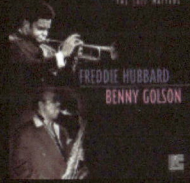
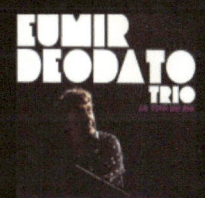

Visit digital.waxpoetics.com/playlist
for our ten-track mix of this issue.

waxpoetics

17 North Parade presents
A VINTAGE REGGAE PRESENTATION

REGGAE ANTHOLOGY: NINEY THE OBSERVER
ROOTS WITH QUALITY VP 4148

Over The past 3 decades Niney The Observer has produced high quality records with reggae's biggest superstars. This 2 CD retrospective features a long list of Roots Reggae legends, deejay versions and amazing King Tubby's dub mixes in a package that tells the full story of one of the most inventive producers in Jamaican music history.

COMING JAN. 09'

FREDDIE McGREGOR
MR. McGREGOR VP 4149

Freddie McGregor's 1979 debut album produced by Niney The Observer peeked at # 2 on the UK reggae album charts in June 1979. This special edition features 7 bonus tracks and includes 4 showcase discomixes encompassing a major portion of the output between the singer and producer.

COMING JAN. 09'

REGGAE ANTHOLOGY: JOE GIBBS
SCORCHERS FROM THE EARLY YEARS (1967-73) VP 4151

A collection of the amazing Rocksteady & Reggae hits that appeared on the Joe Gibbs' labels in the late 60's and early 70's, performed by a who's who of artists responsible for breaking the sound of Reggae internationally. Produced mainly by Lee 'Scratch' Perry & Niney The Observer for Gibbs, This jam packed 2 CD anthology features special edits only available in this package.

COMING APR. 09'

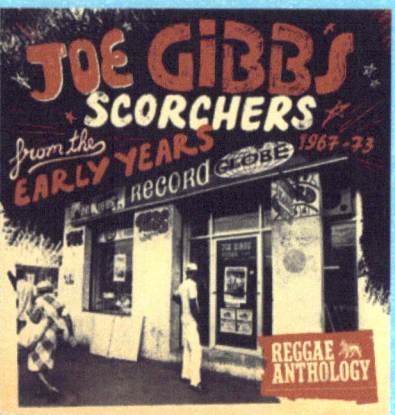

THE HEPTONES
MEET THE NOW GENERATION VP 4152

When originally released in 1972, the Heptones material for Joe Gibbs appeared on two various artists LP's. Here we feature these tracks on a single CD, with the addition of very rare deejay cuts and dubs. The music featured here is recognized as the best from the sublime Heptones after their extended stay at Studio One

COMING APR. 09'

POWER HOUSE SELECTOR'S CHOICE:
GEORGE PHANG VP 4150

2 LP set featuring a selection of George Phang's biggest hits. 28 tracks on 14 of the most popular riddims released on his Power House label.

ALSO AVAILABLE
THE COMPLETE POWER HOUSE SELECTOR'S CHOICE (8 CD'S 160 TRACKS)

COMING FEB. 09'

www.17northparade.com — www.planetreggae.com — www.vpreggae.com

TEST YOUR REGGAE KNOWLEDGE!

 Name three of Niney the Observer's biggest hits.

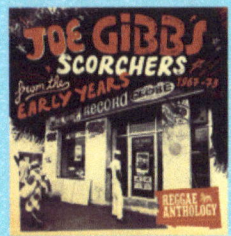 What reggae movie did Joe Gibbs make a cameo?

 Who were the two musicians George Phang used to create the bulk of his riddims, also known as the "Riddim Twins?"

Rope in and test your Reggae knowledge!
17 North Parade presents
VINTAGE REGGAE TRIVIA!

Winners will receive a vinyl gift pack of vintage 12" and 7" Reggae singles.

For official contest rules:
www.VPRECORDS.com/VintageTrivia.vp

WWW.17NORTHPARADE.COM – WWW.PLANETREGGAE.COM – WWW.VPREGGAE.COM

www.WaxPoetics.com

OUT NOW WORLDWIDE

Available with limited edition Guilty Simpson/Oh No Fan Club 45 (Stones Throw/Now-Again) at these retail stores:

USA: Turntable Lab, Dusty Groove, giantpeach.com, undergroundhiphop.com, Access Music, Amoeba Records, 360 Vinyl, Reckless Records, Twist & Shout, Easy Street, Other Music, Love Garden, Ear X Tacy, Park Avenue.

Canada: Play De Record, Beat Street

Europe: Fat City, Soul Jazz, juno.co.uk, kingunderground.com, HHV.de, Rush Hour, Hum Records

Japan: Jazzy Sport.

www.nowagainrecords.com

waxpoetics digital

digital.waxpoetics.com

PERFORMANCE QUALITY MP3s
FREE TRACK EVERY WEEK

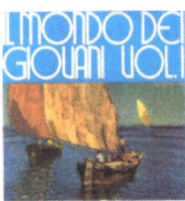   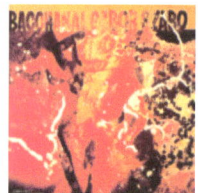

SEE THE ICON. GET THE MUSIC.

The Lyman Woodard Organization
"saturday night special"

On Sale Now

Saturday Night Special, the fifth release by Wax Poetics Records, comes in the wake of Lyman Woodard's recent and untimely passing at the youthful age of sixty-six. To commemorate his magnum opus, Wax Poetics Records releases *Saturday Night Special* as a 180-gram double LP, limited to 1,500 numbered copies and featuring original liner notes by John Sinclair, new interviews, never-before-seen photos, and a replica of the original promotional poster. The iconic cover photograph, "The Equalizers" taken by Detroit's Leni Sinclair, has been presented in its original form.

waxpoeticsrecords

GREAT JAZZ IS MADE ON impulse!

CELEBRATING THE LEGACY OF JOHN COLTRANE AND THE JAZZ LEGENDS FROM THE IMMORTAL IMPULSE RECORDS LABEL

• CLASSICS FROM JOHN COLTRANE

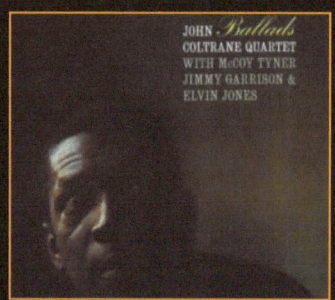
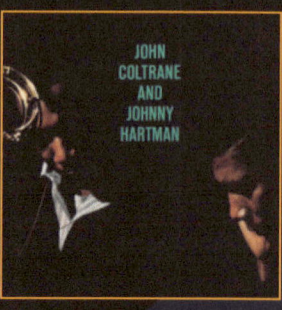

A LOVE SUPREME
A suite about redemption, a work of pure spirit and song, that encapsulates all the struggles and aspirations of the 1960s.

BALLADS
The classic collection of both well known and obscure ballads.

JOHN COLTRANE & JOHNNY HARTMAN
The masterpiece from 1963.

• VARIOUS ARTISTS
THE HOUSE THAT TRANE BUILT
THE STORY OF IMPULSE RECORDS

The 4-CD collection features 38 label-defining tracks from the Impulse vaults, from Oliver Nelson's "Stolen Moments" to John Coltrane's "Acknowledgement" (from *A Love Supreme*) to Pharoah Sanders' "The Creator Has A Master Plan."

• ALSO AVAILABLE
10 SINGLE-DISC BEST-OF TITLES FROM THE FOLLOWING IMPULSE ARTISTS

John Coltrane

Albert Ayler

McCoy Tyner

Charles Mingus

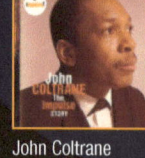
Sonny Rollins

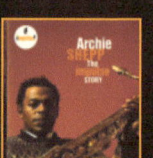
Archie Shepp

Pharoah Sanders

Alice Coltrane

Gato Barbieri

Keith Jarrett

AVAILABLE AT amazon.com

© 2009 Universal Music Enterprises, a Division of UMG Recordings, Inc.

waxpoetics №**34**

EDITOR'S LETTER	13
RE:DISCOVERY	16
IN MEMORIAM	26
9DW	34
STONEPHACE	36
ULULATION	38
MELVIN SPARKS	44
HORACE TAPSCOTT	52
RICHARD EVANS	64
CREED TAYLOR	76
JOEL DORN	100
ANALOG OUT	112

Front Cover
John Coltrane
photography **Francis Wolff** © Mosaic Images

Back Cover
Freddie Hubbard
photography **Chuck Stewart**

joyous shout!

Chico Hamilton looks back not as a summation but with the past as a jumping off point to where he is now; the foundation to build off of what he has to say in the here and now. This album has Chico writing for and playing with an enlarged ensemble, offering us a glimpse of his life's journey and some of those he has shared it with. It speaks greatly of all the musicians' skills that they are performing Chico's compositions yet their interplay becomes another color on his palette, which allows him to further embellish the picture he is painting. This is one of the appealing aspects to all of Chico's music, an always-organic sense of tension and release. Guest spots include trombonist George Bohanon, who was in one of Chico's classic sixties ensembles; vocalist Jose James, who studied under Chico at The New School's Jazz and Contemporary Music program; and multi-reedist Jack Kelso, Chico's lifelong friend. This album is a celebration of a lifelong romance Chico has had with music and the relationships that came into his life both past and present through his service to the muse. Those who forge their own way may travel a harder road but their art loses none of its power with the passage of time because of these trials. "Twelve Tones of Love" is proof of that aphorism to continuously enjoy.

From the liner notes by
Maxwell Chandler

Twelve Tones of Love: JS10012
Release Date: 4/14/09

joyousshout.com
www.myspace.com/chico hamilton

distributed by redeyeusa.com

waxpoetics

WAX POETICS, INC.
45 Main Street, Suite 224
Brooklyn, NY 11201
p 866.999.4WAX
p 718.624.5696
f 718.624.5695
info@waxpoetics.com
waxpoetics.com

ADVERTISE
advertise@waxpoetics.com
or call 718.624.5696 x203

SUBSCRIBE
waxpoetics.com/subscribe
subscribe@waxpoetics.com

RETAIL
retail@waxpoetics.com
or contact Melanie Raucci,
Disticor Magazine
Distribution Services, at
631.587.1160
mraucci@disticor.com

CONTRIBUTE
editorial@waxpoetics.com

Editor-in-Chief
Andre Torres

Editor
Brian DiGenti

Marketing Director
Dennis Coxen

Copy Editor
Tom McClure
Associate Editor
Jon Kirby

Art Directors
Joshua Dunn
Freddy Allen Anzures

Operations Manager
Richard Smith
Sales Manager
Michael Coxen
Sales Associates
Paul Alexander
Ben Arsenault
Record Label Manager
Amir Abdullah
Accounts Receivable
Connie S. Reale

Interns
Christopher Arena
Corey Galotta
Jonathan Gelatt
Chris Hund
Alex Rhea
Everett Saunders
Chaya Wilkins

Contributing Editors
Dante Carfagna
John Paul Jones
Andrew Mason
Matt Rogers

Contributing Writers
Chris Arena
Andy Beta
Robbie Busch
Seb Carayol
Bill Carbone
Jonathan Gelatt
Duane Harriott
Jon Kirby
Peter Kirn
John Kruth
Devin Leonard
David Ma
Kristofer Ríos
Andy Thomas
Dan Ubick

Contributing Photo Editor
B+

Contributing Photographers
Kamau Daáood
Peter Flutter
Andrew Lepley
Roberto Polillo
Faye Rosendorn
Leni Sinclair
Chuck Stewart
Mark Weber
Michael Dett Wilcots

Published by **Wax Poetics, Inc.**
Printed by **MGM Printing Group**
Distributed by **Disticor Magazine Distribution Services**

© 2009 Wax Poetics, Inc.
All rights reserved. Unauthorized duplication without prior consent is prohibited. ISSN 1537-8241

waxpoetics N° 34

I've talked about my grandfather before; he and my father have always been my musical mentors. Their passion for music was infectious, and I caught the bug early on. Between the two of them, I was pretty much exposed to all of the great music in my life. So jazz wasn't something out of the ordinary or strange to me as a kid growing up. My pops used to tell me stories about how, as a teen, he and his boys would get together to play jazz records and just party—to jazz. I witnessed firsthand the power of the music, as I was fortunate enough to spend many hours with my grandfather. Having grown up running packages for the real gangsters in Italian Harlem (before it became known as Spanish Harlem), my grandfather was a real old-school jazz head. I can remember his ritual of getting a beer, turning off the TV, and sitting down in "his" chair staring straight ahead at the stereo, completely engaged as Jackie McLean traded eights with Webster Young.

This is what jazz meant to me as a young kid, and by the time I was in junior high, I was checking out Jaco Pastorius cassettes from the public library. But high school mostly meant a steady supply of hip-hop, rock, and pop, and it wasn't until college that I would really dig deeper into jazz. But when I did, I never turned back. Today, jazz is the music of a small minority, with most people hanging onto limiting definitions of the music, while others have drained the life out if and turned it into smooth background drivel. But here at Wax Poetics, we still have much love for jazz. And while we do show respect to the more traditional side, we're mostly attracted to the often-maligned funkier side of jazz. This is the side that delivered the joints that got our attention in the '90s because of cats like DJ Premier and Pete Rock flipping them into hip-hop classics.

While we've featured more than our fair share of jazz heroes, this is the first time we've devoted an entire issue to them. In typical fashion, we've kept it left of center and anything but traditional, providing a range of legends, both known and unknown. While Coltrane graces the cover, it's Creed Taylor who stands front and center. If there was ever someone who's taken the heat for funky jazz, it's this genius producer extraordinaire. Sure, the purists will give him credit for his work at Verve and founding Impulse, even for blowing up bossa nova in the States, but when it comes to CTI, they're not really riding with him. But ask any real head, and they'll quickly tell you that without classic tracks like "Take Me to the Mardi Gras" or "Nautilus," hip-hop just wouldn't be the same. So we give Creed his props, because even if they didn't get it then, we get it now. CTI isn't just about the music, it's the complete package. From the meticulous production to the inspired photography and design, Creed Taylor knew what he wanted, and it worked. The label put out some of the most distinctive jazz music of the last century and sold a lot of records in the process.

So it's Creed who leads this issue's Band of Outsiders, a group of jazz rebels who worked against the grain, following their singular vision and moving the music forward. We get the opportunity to talk with Richard Evans about his distinct brand of soul-jazz at Cadet, have a final conversation with Joel Dorn about his golden period at Atlantic, and dig into Horace Tapscott's Los Angeles spiritual jazz collective, the Pan Afrikan Peoples Arkestra. Each one of these innovators redefined jazz by following their gut, some calculating tremendous commercial success selling millions, others content merely reaching the local community.

We like to occupy the space somewhere in the middle, building our community of dedicated followers into legions of Wax Poetics evangelists preaching the good word throughout the land. So your favorite band of outsiders continues its tradition of providing nothing but the best in music history. It's getting greasier by the day out there, but rest assured that we'll be here grinding away on the low throughout this economic trough.

The recession's not the only thing on our mind; it's been a bit emotional over the last month with the passing of a couple of individuals that were very much a part of the Wax Poetics family. We had grown close to Lyman Woodard while working on the reissue of his seminal *Saturday Night Special* LP when he unexpectedly passed just a month shy of its release. He will be sorely missed, yet his music lives on for eternity. Even closer to home has been the passing of John Joseph Nevins II, the father of Wax Poetics family member Amir Abdullah and a big inspiration and source of jazz knowledge throughout Amir's life. His presence has been indirectly felt by many through his son, and will continue to live on. It is in his memory that we dedicate this issue.

They say in death comes life, and that's comforting to know. I can rest reassured it's all going to be all right when thinking about my own sons. When a classmate's mother asked him what kind of music he likes, my oldest son Miles instinctively responded, "Jazz!" Now that's what I'm talking about.

Don't stop the groove,

Andre Torres

waxpoetics®
PREMIUM SUBSCRIPTION

Same price as newsstand
Shipped quickly via USPS First Class Mail
Protected in secure cardboard mailer
Upgrades available for current subscribers

waxpoetics.com/subscribe

Service for U.S. customers only. For subscription questions, email subscribe@waxpoetics.com.

waxpoetics storefront

we got the jazz at waxpoetics.com

Records
The Lyman Woodard Organization
Melvyn Price
The Five Corners Quintet
Auteur Jazz

Apparel
Friend or Foe
Gama
Wax Poetics
Ubiquity

DVDs
Jazz Icons series
David Axelrod
Charles Mingus
Sun Ra

Back Issues
Weldon Irvine (Issue 3)
David Axelrod (Issue 14)
Miles Davis (Issue 25)
Herbie Hancock (Issue 29)

waxpoetics.com/storefront

re:Discovery

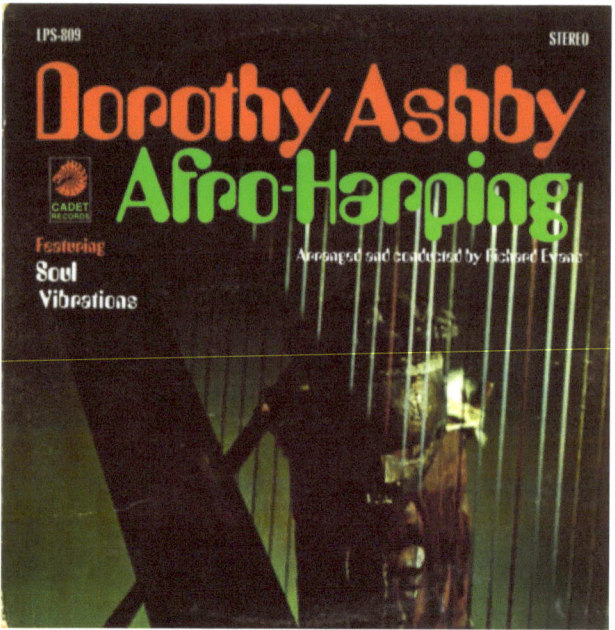

DOROTHY ASHBY

Afro-Harping
(Cadet) 1968

With the first pulse of "Soul Vibrations," Dorothy Ashby sweeps you up with a single glissando of her harp into another dimension of sound. Laconic strings waft as the rhythm section runs the voodoo down, and a disembodied theremin ululates like an electronic banshee. Ashby's music is all about atmosphere—more Blackspace/lounge/bachelor-pad soundtrack than the soul-searching improvisations of the spiritual jazz era. Producer Richard Evans's short, well-crafted arrangements don't lend themselves to extended flights of sonic fancy; the songs range from three to four minutes tops, with barely a note wasted.

Mixing up this gorgeous sonic marmalade is guitarist Phil Upchurch, bassist Richard Davis, drummer Grady Tate, and percussionist Willie Bobo, among others. Unfortunately, the lesser-known musicians were omitted from the original liner notes, as well as later editions of the record. As the credits simply state: "Others unknown."

Ashby, although below the public's radar, was greatly admired by her fellow musicians and in great demand as a session player. The whoosh of her transcendental harp can be heard on songs by Stevie Wonder; Earth, Wind & Fire; Bill Withers; and Dionne Warwick, to name a few.

The title track, a driving soul vamp, features some deep-pocket drumming, Willie Bobo's congas, and a funky bass line that support Ms. Ashby's gentle pluck. "Life Has Its Trials," with its syncopated bass line and a chorus of horns punctuating the brief solos, recalls John Coltrane's driving waltz arrangement of "Greensleeves" from his classic *Africa/Brass* sessions. Richard Evans's lush and delicious arrangements include fresh interpretations of Burt Bacharach's "The Look of Love," André Previn's "Theme from *Valley of the Dolls*," and Neal Hefti's "Lonely Girl" from the film *Harlow*.

Recorded during the Vietnam War's Tet Offensive (late January–February 1968), *Afro-Harping* must have been something of a sonic salve to a very turbulent and troubled time. Revolution was in the air, and both Evans and Cadet Records were clearly at a creative peak, creating unclassifiable music in 1968 (which also saw the release of the much-maligned, psychedelic revamp of Muddy Waters' oeurve, *Electric Mud*). Now, a little over thirty years later, the angelic tonality of Ashby's instrument still has a truly soul-soothing effect. ○ **John Kruth**

STEREO PRESENTS...

We are proud to announce the official re-release of Stereo's legendary films, "A Visual Sound" and "Tincan Folklore". Originally released in 1994 and 1996 respectively, these timeless classics are available for the first time ever on DVD.

"A Visual Sound" features original music by Ululation. Album coming soon on Wax Poetics Records.

featuring riders:
Carl Shipman
Mike Daher
Greg Hunt
Matt Rodriguez
Chris Pastras
Mike Frazier
Neville Sandzabar
Ethan Fowler
& Jason Lee

The 2 disc box set includes director's commentary from Co-Captain's Jason Lee and Chris Pastras.
Available at finer skateshops everywhere.
Enjoy!

STEREO   WWW.STEREOSOUNDAGENCY.COM

re:Discovery

AL WILLIAMS QUINTET PLUS ONE

Sandance
(Renaissance Records) 1976

If you're a New Yorker, the first time you dip your toes in the Pacific Ocean is a magical experience. You may not believe it, you may not want it to happen, but the alien sway of the Western waters does transform you. A sense of new possibilities opens up, and the chill of the East washes away—if only for a moment.

The best live sets captured on wax always have this transformative power. There is an ease of knowingness that runs through a combo that's imbued with a sense of simpatico. Drummer Al Williams leads his crew of seasoned sidemen (Dwight Dickerson, piano; Charles Owens, tenor sax; Nolan Smith, trumpet; Leroy Vinnegar, bass; and Victor Cardenas, percussion) through this set, recorded over three days in the summer of '76 in Long Beach, California, with such an assured hand that you feel the power of the sun and sand inside every groove. The waves lap at you as the swell of notes draws you in.

They kick things off with the title cut, "Sandance," a breakbeat-propelled blast of funk in the sunshine. The horns join the party, jump into the surf, and slide back to shore for their powerful solos as the rhythm section keeps the heat on high. The majority of the cuts are original tunes penned by various members of the band. They roll through an easygoing selection of modern jazz that draws so much inspiration from the nearby beach that you can smell the saltwater. The fact that they were all playing acoustic instruments helps solidify the slightly sun-baked sound and gives every note an air of nostalgia.

As the tide comes in, the group hits a high-water mark with their take on the Leon Russell classic "This Masquerade"—a warm wind that blows with the promise of things to come. And now that they've left it on the stage, they launch headfirst into John Coltrane's "Impressions." As if they were trying to rebuild the very essence of music, they attack like a laughing ocean and erode the shore so that they can dance in the sand—unencumbered and renewed. ○ **Robbie Busch**

livewired
PLUG INTO THE ELECTRIC UNDERGROUND

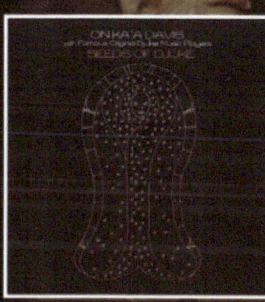

On *Ancients Speak*, bassist and producer **Melvin Gibbs** and his **Elevated Entity** collective tap into a Black Atlantic Continuum stretching from New York to Bahia and beyond. Special guests include John Medeski, Pete Cosey, Blackbyrd McKnight, Amayo from Antibalas and co-producers Arto Lindsay and Kassin.

Conducted by Greg Tate, **Burnt Sugar the Arkestra Chamber** propels *Bitches Brew* further into the 21st century with *Making Love to the Dark Ages*, featuring Jared Michael Nickerson (bass), Vijay Iyer (piano), Lewis "Flip" Barnes Jr. (trumpet), Lisala (vocals), Swiss Chris (drums) and Vernon Reid (guitar).

Fueled by love, faith and the ecstatic energy of straight-up diva soul, singer and composer **M. Nahadr** crafts Afro-futuristic fusions of funk, jazz, dance and electronics on her sky-touching debut *EclecticIsM*. Co-produced by Grammy Award winner James P. Nichols.

Virtuoso guitarist **On Ka'a Davis** is a true vet of Sun Ra's Arkestra (with Sun Ra himself)—experience that informs *Seeds Of Djuke's* heady brew. Joined by drummer Jojo Kuo (Fela, Manu Dibango), bassist Francis Mbappe and a host of fellow travelers, Davis paints a multi-hued canvas of free-jazz Afrobeat and funky spirituality.

IN STORES MARCH 17

IN STORES APRIL 21

Empowering artists. Building communities. Better together.

www.livewiredmusic.org

re:Discovery

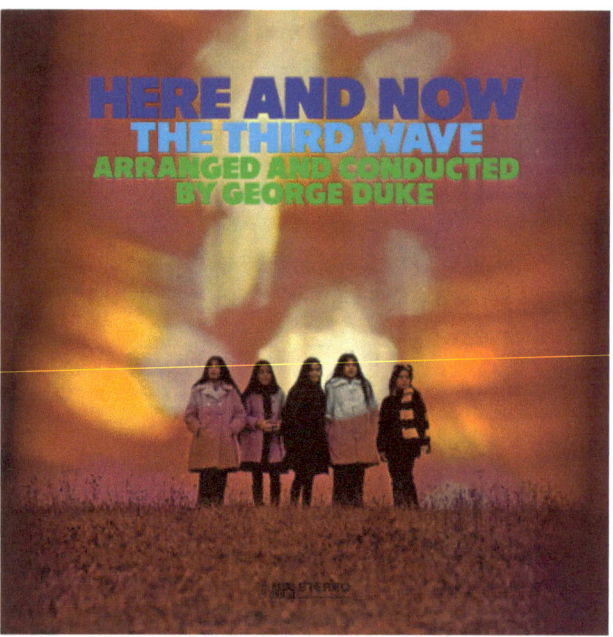

THE THIRD WAVE

Here and Now
(MPS Records) 1970

The Third Wave, comprised of five teenage Filipino sisters from Stockton, California, were introduced to bandleader George Duke by West Coast jazz figure Flip Nuñez. Duke, then in his early twenties, heard the harmonizing sisters and immediately began performing with them throughout the Bay Area with his own trio. *Here and Now*, the group's lone recording, would never see a stateside release.

Upon first listen, one could say that it's a solid, cool, and easy vocal jazz record—a substantial contribution to the sunny, psych-jazz-pop aesthetic popularly depicted by the Free Design, Sergio Mendes, and Quarteto em Cy. On *Here and Now*, the Third Wave bop through charming and enthusiastic covers of "Cantaloupe Island," "Got to Get You Into My Life," and "Stormy"—renditions that would garner blue ribbons in any high school swing choir competition. George Duke's surprisingly subtle vocal and brass arrangements deftly balance bossa and American swing, serving as an early indication of the Brazilian-flavored jazz fusion he would create years later.

After subsequent listens, the astonishingly fragile beauty of this record really starts to reveal itself. Although the sisters' teenaged voices had not yet fully matured, you can't hear a trace of unruly vibrato in their pitch-perfect harmonies. The girls strain to hit the sophisticated Technicolor changes of "Maiden Voyage," singing the rarely heard lyrics penned by Herbie's sister, Jean Hancock. The timbre and unified phrasing that the Third Wave achieved on this record could only have come from a lifetime of familial singing.

What makes this album so special is that there aren't too many pure and honest examples of youthful exuberance in vocal jazz from this era. Most records of this ilk were made by older, more established jazz artists who used this hybrid as a halfhearted attempt to stay relevant in an ever-changing musical landscape. What you're actually listening to is a vocal jazz record for young people, made by young people who truly loved jazz and loved singing it together.

Although this collaboration would be the start of Duke's industrious partnership with Germany's MPS Records, the Third Wave is probably most notable in the Duke family for spawning a much more significant partnership. Shortly after meeting the sisters, Josie Cannon, the mother of the singing teens, introduced George to Corine—now his wife of thirty-eight years. ● **Duane Harriott**

JAKE ONE *"WHITE VAN MUSIC"* - CD / 2LP (limited white vinyl)
Debut album from Seattle super producer Jake One featuring **MF DOOM**, **Little Brother**, **M.O.P.**, **Slug**, **Prodigy**, **Posdnuos**, **Busta Rhymes**, **Freeway**, **Brother Ali**, **Young Buck**, **Alchemist**, **Evidence**, **Casual**, **Keak Da Sneak**, **Black Milk**, **Royce Da 5'9"**, **eLZhi**, **Bishop Lamont**, **Blueprint** and more. Initial pressing includes a Free bonus disc featuring instrumentals.

www.myspace.com/jakeone | www.jakeone.com

ATMOSPHERE *"GODLOVESUGLY"* - CD+DVD / 2LP+DVD (Re-Issue)
The critically acclaimed third official studio album from **Slug** & **Ant** is back and uglier than ever. Remastered and repackaged, the *Godlovesugly* re-issue also includes the ultra rare *Sad Clown Bad Dub 4 (The Godlovesugly Release Parties) DVD* that features 2 hours of live performance footage, backstage shenanigans, several special guest appearances and music videos for *"Godlovesugly"*, *"Summersong"* and *"Say Shhh"*.

www.myspace.com/atmosphere | www.youresugly.com

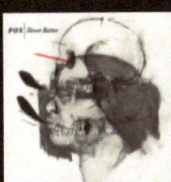

P.O.S *"NEVER BETTER"* - CD / 2LP (limited clear vinyl)
P.O.S returns with the follow up to 2006's *Audition*. The limited initial pressing of *Never Better* is packaged in a limited clear custom digi-pak that features 22 solid and transparent inserts to create your own cover art combinations.

"P.O.S has saved Hip Hop...Never Better is amazing and likely to be the best Hip Hop album of 2009." -Alarm

www.myspace.com/pos | www.rhymesayers.com/neverbetter

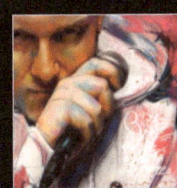

BROTHER ALI *"THE TRUTH IS HERE"* - CD+DVD / 2LP+DVD
9 previously unreleased and new tracks from **Ali** & **Ant** to hold your over until the new album drops Fall '09. Also includes a full-length DVD featuring the Sold Out homecoming performance from *The Undisputed Truth Tour* at First Avenue, as well as bonus commentary and music videos.

IN STORES 3.10.09

www.myspace.com/brotherali | www.brotherali.com

ABSTRACT RUDE *"REJUVENATION"* - CD / 2LP
West coast legend, ATU, Massmen, Project Blowed, Haiku D'Etat, and A-Team affiliate **Abstract Rude** re-emerges with *Rejuvenation*. Produced entirely by Seattle super producer **Vitamin D** (*G-Unit, Redman, Gift of Gab, etc*) *Rejuvenation* is a hard hitting soulful ryde showcasing Ab Rude's distinct and unlimited vocal stylings.

IN STORES 5.05.09

www.myspace.com/abstractrude

COMING SOON:
FREEWAY + JAKE ONE "THE STIMULUS PACKAGE"- CD/2LP
SOUNDSET '08 - CD/DVD
TOKI WRIGHT "A DIFFERENT MIRROR" - CD
EYEDEA & ABILITIES "BY THE THROAT" - CD/2LP
BLUEPRINT "ADVENTURES IN COUNTER CULTURE" - CD/2LP
I SELF DEVINE "THE SOUND OF LOW CLASS AMERIKA" - CD/2LP+DVD
BROTHER ALI "THE STREET PREACHER" - CD/2LP
SOUNDSET '09 FESTIVAL - 5.24.09 SHAKOPEE, MN
and more...

get in the know:
www.rhymesayers.com | www.fifthelementonline.com | www.soundsetfestival.com

re:Discovery

SLIPSTREAM

Afterglow
(Bernup Records) 1982

Slipstream was led by reedman Bernie Kenerson, a Florida native who attended Boston's prestigious Berklee College of Music in the late '70s. Although influenced by saxophone greats like John Coltrane and John Klemmer, Kenerson was also enamored with electric-era Miles and similar jazz mutations of the decade. Seeking to generate a new sound of his own, Bernie purchased a Lyricon, the world's first wind-powered synthesizer, directly from inventor Bill Bernardi's factory in nearby Brockton, Massachusetts.

In 1981, Kenerson retreated to Boone, North Carolina, where he enrolled at Appalachian State University, assembling Slipstream from a musical cast of mustachioed locals. Taking fusion cues from Spyro Gyra and Return to Forever, *Afterglow* was a mixture of straightahead and far-beyond compositions, with Kenerson alternating between soprano, alto, and electric sax. On "She Said," Kenerson's camp treats listeners to a night in Tunisia spent racing go-carts around the abandoned Atari factory. Although the early '80s were notoriously unkind to jazz, songs like "Spindry" and "Summer Release" crank up the nitrous of smooth jazz's dentist-office aesthetic, rendering a product that simulates Bob James in zero gravity. With a primarily organic rhythm section of Fender Rhodes, fretless electric bass, drums, and percussion, Kenerson's Lyricon forces this rural Weather Report's collective sound through a retrofitted filter of futuristic feel. As an admirer of fusion's aggressive guitarists, Kenerson's manic leads often resemble an expert-level Guitar Hero composite of "Giant Steps" and the theme from *Night Court*. A result of *Afterglow*'s triple-digit pressing on Bernie's own cleverly eponymous Bernup Records, the album soon earned Slipstream a Student Recording Award from *Down Beat* magazine.

On the strength of *Afterglow*, Slipstream was booked for the 1982 World's Fair in Knoxville, Tennessee, where an international audience was introduced to the slinky sounds of the Lyricon, the exotic taste of Cherry Coke, and the convenience of dehydrated milk. Although a midseason dismissal from a six-month residency in Clearwater, Florida, would dissolve Slipstream's classic incarnation, Kenerson still performs many of the songs featured on this privately pressed pearl with the Bernie Kenerson Group. Although Bernie still owns his Lyricon—one of three hundred handmade models that predate Selmer's mass-produced Lyricon II—he now serenades the smooth-jazz masses with the Akai EWI via his *Art of the EWI* series and constant touring throughout the Southeast. ● **Jon Kirby**

re:Discovery

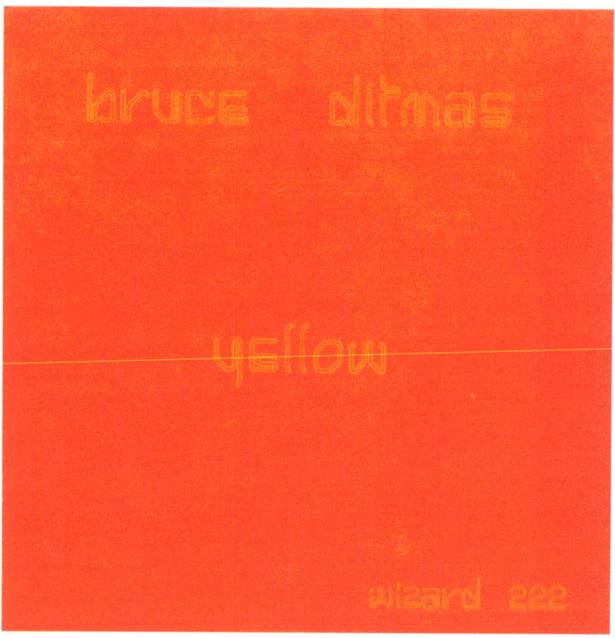

BRUCE DITMAS
Yellow
(Wizard Records) 1977

The name Bruce tends to hang around my family tree: it's my youngest uncle's name, my mother's second husband's name, not to mention her favorite Super Bowl halftime performer. While mining a vein of odd records that wound up in an antiques mall in South Texas (including hand-painted synth records, Italo no-wave 12-inches, and French electroacoustic LPs with the 3-D glasses attached, all with the original Wax Trax price tags still affixed), I naturally gravitated towards one in a glowing red sleeve with "Bruce Ditmas" and "Yellow" written in a kinked wire font. If the long-haired beardo in Cazals cast in yellow wasn't enticing enough, then his array of gear was: drums, Moog drum, Minimoog synthesizer, ARP 2600 synthesizer, electric congas, cuíca, percussion.

The Atlantic City–born Ditmas backed everyone from Judy Garland and Babs to Chet Baker and Lee Konitz, even appearing on Jaco Pastorius's *Jaco* album from 1974. Around 1976–77, he began dabbling in electronics and drum machines in earnest, collaborating intently with abstract vocalist Joan La Barbara (the future Mrs. Morton Subotnick). On his own, Ditmas was no doubt digging the fault line between jazz chop-shop noodling and proto-techno klingklang, all in the shadow of Mt. Patrick Gleeson.

Released in 1977 by Wizard Records (responsible for another Ditmas record, a mesmeric flute album by Carl Stone, and two early La Barbara efforts), Bruce extends thanks to "Trevor and Kim's foot," though true gratitude goes to guests La Barbara and ECM trumpeter Enrico Rava. Opening cut "Surprise Hotel" was written by Rava and is his lone appearance. It's also the busiest, most jazzbo cut, with La Barbara on "voice with instant flanger" (though "batshit chitter" is more sonically correct). "L'Unita"—with its wiggle, gurgle, twitter, and spurt—could be spliced into a half-dozen decent disco edits. As is, it uncannily mixes well with Paul McCartney's similarly navel-gazing synth doodle, "Temporary Secretary."

On the second side is where Ditmas relaxes his jazz muscle and does deeper exploratory work. He references Fritz Lang on the minimal "Dr. Mabuse," while the sprawling "Aural Suspension" combines his analog wow with drum-break butter. "Soweto" remains a singular concoction though: crawling through La Barbara's Afro-alien mewl, Bruce slows down what sounds like Ann Peebles's rain blops until it feels like cough syrup. **O** Andy Beta

Lyman with his son Lyman III; photo by Leni Sinclair

LYMAN WOODARD

1942–2009

Don't Stop the Groove

Although enlightened music fans the world over were saddened by the passing of organist Lyman Woodard, the relationship that Wax Poetics had formed with the gifted musician and composer made the news especially hard to swallow. While orchestrating the comprehensive rerelease of the Lyman Woodard Organization's magnum opus, *Saturday Night Special*, we had grown close to not only Lyman, but to Organization members Ron English and Leonard King, plus a host of others whose artistic efforts helped bring this legendary record to life. With each exchange, Lyman's corner of Detroit, past and present, became part of our own world; with each conversation, more of Michigan's fascinating musical history unfurled before us. Although Lyman had been harboring a notorious cough since the '80s, his declining health made us especially nervous after a fall resulted in seven broken ribs. Although *Saturday Night Special*'s release date was on the horizon, many of us feared Lyman would not be with us to celebrate. A month shy of *Saturday Night Special*'s rebirth, Lyman Woodard passed away at the age of sixty-six.

Lyman displayed a propensity towards music early in life, taking instruction with the organist of the Congregational Church in his hometown of Owosso, Michigan. By high school, Lyman's rampant fascination with R&B music had manifested itself in his playing, which he did in increasing capacity, gigging in nearby Flint. "He was known all over as the kid who could play all the Little Richard piano solos note for note—even the mistakes!" reflected poet/activist John Sinclair, who penned the liner notes to *Saturday Night Special*'s 1975 release. Although the piano was Lyman's first love, he soon fell for the Hammond B-3 after Jimmy Smith's virtuosic playing caused the impressionable player to swerve across several lanes of traffic to keep Smith's sweet serenade within his radio's reception. "I kind of liken the experience to St. Paul being blinded by the truth of Christ," Woodard later remarked.

Woodard's versatility afforded him limitless opportunities in and around Motown, gaining him access to nearly every dimension of Detroit's intricate music scene. Between raucous residencies at Detroit's fabled Frolic Show Bar and J.J.'s Lounge, Woodard would work as bandleader for such marquee attractions as Martha Reeves and the Vandellas as well as Holland-Dozier-Holland darlings, the 8th Day. Lyman was loved by Black and White factions alike, creating an identity that, like his revered Charles Mingus, lacked a distinct racial stamp. "Lyman never told me he was White until 1996," states *Saturday Night Special* drummer Leonard King. Having played off and on with Woodard throughout his career, King duly notes that, beyond race, Woodard's audience transcended societal and generational boundaries as well.

"When we used to play at Cobb's Corner," King says, "I'd look out into the audience, and there'd be people wearing full-length minks sitting next to young people in cutoff jeans. There's something about his music that's just regenerative. And Lyman didn't feel that what he was playing was jazz or blues or rock. He and I shared a similar attitude toward music—that as many colors as we can possibly use to execute this music to the fullest extent, that's what we went for."

Per Lyman's request, King organized a tribute concert to honor Woodard and acknowledge the lasting impression he has made on both Detroit and on his peer performers. "If there's anything I got from him directly," King continues, "it is just to speak honestly; don't tell any lies through the music. He was a beautiful human being and an honest person, and I believe his music speaks of that." ○ **Jon Kirby**

SAVATH SAVALAS LA LLAMA

SAVATH & SAVALAS
(PREFUSE 73) *LA LLAMA*
MADLIB
BEAT KONDUCTA 5 & 6
MAYER HAWTHORNE
THAT HEART RECORD

WWW.STONESTHROW.COM

photo by Michael Ochs Archive/Getty Images

HANK CRAWFORD

1934–2009

Soul Tone

Considering all the jubilation over Obama's inauguration, the month of January '09 turned out to be rather eerie. Beginning on the fifteenth, Ray Charles's baritone saxophonist, Leroy "Hog" Cooper, died at age eighty after a heart attack. Just five days later, multi-reed man David "Fathead" Newman passed away on January 20 following a battle with pancreatic cancer. Then on January 29, Hank Crawford "got his hat" at his Memphis home, after years of poor health following a stroke in 2000. He was seventy-four.

Born December 21, 1934, Bennie Ross Crawford Jr. came up playing piano at his local church in Memphis until his father, a truck driver and frustrated musician, presented him with an alto sax. Bennie soon became known as "Hank" in honor of Hank O'Day, as his tone bore a strong resemblance to that of the local saxophonist. Crawford majored in music theory at Tennessee State and was fronting his own jump-blues band known as Little Hank and the Rhythm Kings (in which he sang and played alto) when Ray rolled into town, in need of someone to fill Hog Cooper's bari chair for the night. A few months later, after Hog quit, Crawford dropped out of school and hit the road full time with Charles's legendary small band.

"Hank was to Ray as Strayhorn was to Duke," Joel Dorn, who produced Crawford's Atlantic sides, once told me. "There was a genuine telepathy between them. At first, Ray would dictate the charts to him off the top of his head, but after a while, Hank just wrote them on his own. He knew what Ray wanted and how the band was supposed to sound. He didn't need Ray to spell it out for him. So not only did he write the arrangements, but he wound up leading Ray's band as well."

Before switching back to alto sax, his main horn since his days at Manassas High (whose jazz band produced stellar saxophonists Charles Lloyd and George Coleman as well as pianist Harold Mabern), Crawford's baritone could be heard rear-guarding classic Ray Charles numbers like "I've Got a Woman," "Drown in My Own Tears," and "What'd I Say."

After leaving Ray in 1963, Hank's records for Atlantic featured his brilliant arrangements and transcendental ballads with a pianoless septet. Crawford signed with Creed Taylor's Kudu label in 1972 and recorded for Milestone a decade later. His best-loved compositions include "Whispering Grass," "The Peeper," and "From the Heart."

Hank's horn was also featured on sides by B. B. King, Etta James, and Eric Clapton, as well as organist Jimmy McGriff, Dr. John, and his bandmate and soul brother David "Fathead" Newman.

"It's very bizarre how all three of those guys passed at once. It makes you wonder if there wasn't some kind of master plan," says David Sanborn, whose signature tone on the alto was inspired by Crawford. Sanborn was just eleven years old when he first saw the Ray Charles band in his hometown of St. Louis. "Both of those guys, Hank and Fathead, were integral to Ray's sound. Seeing them was a visceral experience. They opened the door and turned on the lights. I had polio when I was three and in an iron lung for a year and paralyzed from the neck down for a year after that. The muscles in my left arm had atrophied, so I took up the saxophone as therapy. Then I saw Hank, and that was it. He was the catalyst. He really gave me my life. He had such an emotional directness to his playing, such simplicity and elegance. There was never a wasted note." ○ **John Kruth**

 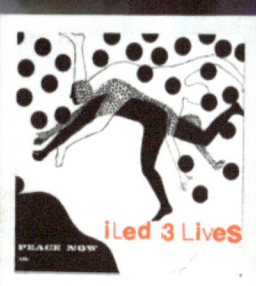 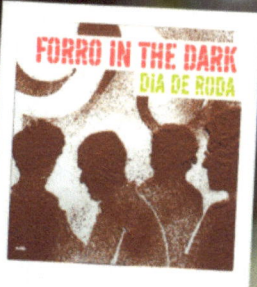 

photo by Leni Sinclair

DAVID "FATHEAD" NEWMAN

1933-2009

Lone Star Legend

Texas, the Dallas/Fort Worth area in particular, has given birth to a long tradition of great tenor saxophonists—Arnett Cobb, King Curtis, Ornette Coleman (who began on tenor), Booker Ervin, and Dewey Redman, to name a few. Among this masterful crew was David "Fathead" Newman, who passed away on January 20, 2009, in Kingston, New York, after battling pancreatic cancer. He was seventy-five.

"My mentor was Buster Smith, and there was Red Connors, a bebop man, who was way ahead of his time," Fathead (a nickname thrust upon him by a frustrated high school music teacher) once told me. "I played alto in his group when I first met Ornette Coleman. We were both still in high school. Ornette was playing tenor, and I played alto."

"I loved bebop, but you could never make any money playing it," Newman explained. "To earn money, I backed up [bluesmen] Lowell Fulson and T-Bone Walker for four or five years, playing one-nighters across the South and the Midwest, until I met Ray Charles."

Newman (who Charles dubbed "Brains" in lieu of his derogatory moniker) joined Charles in 1954 on baritone but soon switched to tenor, replacing the great Don Wilkerson. Along with his friend, saxophonist/pianist/writer and arranger Hank (Bennie) Crawford, Newman played a key role in Ray's remarkable small band (check out his solo on the live version of "Drown in My Own Tears").

Back in his disc jockey days on Philly jazz station WHAT, Atlantic producer Joel Dorn used Newman's rendition of Paul Mitchell's "Hard Times" (from David's 1958 album as a leader, *Fathead: Ray Charles Presents David Newman*) as his theme song. "It was doin' okay as a jazz album, but it didn't really bust out," Joel told me in 2007. "When I made it my theme song, it started sellin' hundreds of copies a month."

Beyond his original twelve-year stint with Charles and a brief return in 1970, Fathead maintained a solid solo career, recording for Atlantic and Warner Bros. with Dorn usually at the helm, as well as with Prestige and, most recently, High Note Records. Newman's soulful solos soar on songs by Aretha Franklin, Aaron Neville, B. B. King, Natalie Cole, Little Jimmy Scott, and Donny Hathaway.

Michael Cuscuna, who produced two albums by Newman in the early '80s for Muse, recalls Fathead as a "gentle, sincere, and extraordinarily generous" person, as well as a first-class musician. "The character Fathead [played by Bokeem Woodbine] in the film *Ray* was not him. It was a composite. He told the director, 'Don't portray me as the guy who turned Ray on to junk.' And of course, that's exactly what happened. Even after that, he said, 'I'm okay with it.' He thought it was a good film.

"Fathead never played three notes when one would do. He'd just go for the perfect note," Cuscuna points out. "As a doubler [Newman not only played tenor, but soprano, alto, and baritone sax as well as flute], he had a unique, gorgeous tone on all of his instruments."

"He was a beautiful guy," Les McCann recalls. "I worked with Fathead in Herbie Mann's group the Family of Mann. It's unusual to find someone with a tone like that. Women used to say he sounded like he was talkin' to them."

"He's the reason I have a house," trumpeter/arranger Steven Bernstein says. "In a very gentle way, he gave me some real-life advice. After *Kansas City* [the Robert Altman film in which Newman appeared], we were on the road together for three weeks. He was the only older guy in the band, and I was the bandleader. He was very professional, kind, and nice to me. He pulled me aside and said, 'Now that you're making a little money, find a place outside the city that you can afford.' You couldn't find a better musician. He was supreme. He combined bebop, harmonic swing, and soul into a sophisticated, singular voice. You could sing his solos, they were so melodic. From city to city across America, Fathead always got the biggest ovation. People never forgot his work with Ray."

David leaves behind Karen, his wife and manager of twenty-eight years, along with four sons, seven grandchildren, and three great-grandchildren. ● John Kruth

Tru Thoughts recordings

Azaxx
The Exotic Delight Bay
TRUCD185

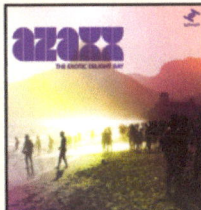

Fusing influences from **Brazil**, **Colombia** and **Latin flavours** with **beats**, **head nod** and **BMore grooves**. Essential DJ music.

9th March

Kinny
Idle Forest Of Chit Chat
TRUCD175

Modern soul music from this powerful and unique singer, with production from **Quantic**, **TM Juke**, **Hint** and **Nostalgia 77**.

23rd March

Nostalgia 77 Sessions
Featuring Keith & Julie Tippett
TRUCD183

Stalwarts of **British jazz** and **soul** hook up with a new generation for this **classically deep** album.

6th April

Stonephace
Stonephace
TRUCD186

Psychedelic hip hop grooves featuring **Adrian Utley (Portishead)**. For fans of **Madlib**, **Natural Yoghurt Band** and **The Heliocentrics**.

20th April

Flevans
27 Devils
TRUCD191

An irresistible, **hook-laden** album packed with **glorious songs** and **dancefloor bombs**.

18th May

Visit www.tru-thoughts.co.uk for all tour dates, releases and news, and listen to our radio shows anytime on www.totallyradio.com

All Tru Thoughts & Zebra Traffic music is available direct from **www.etchshop.co.uk**

9dw
Migrant 12"EP catune-31

This is Extended Mix of "Migrant" included 9dw "Self titled" which was released in 2008. Featured Three Remixers, Ackky, Inner Science and World Famous. San Francisco's "Windsurf" played it on BBC Radio 1 ROB DA BANK's show.

http://www.myspace.com/9dw

Non+ Herrmutt Lobby
ハンター CD CTLR-0006

The album ハンター is a meeting on a mind-scape, hearing lyrics that match wits with the beats in a intellectual intercourse resulting with a electro birth of sound that can only be describe as hip-hop riding a waveform of bass over a torrent of drums and arriving at the shore of uncharted music, in a newly discovered world of sound, known as Non + Herrmut Lobby.

Also available

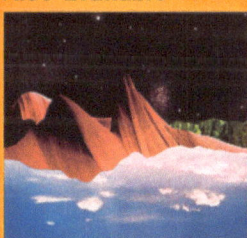

9dw 13 songs CD
catune-30

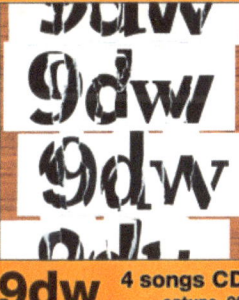

9dw 4 songs CD
catune-29

Upcoming Release
Boris vs 9dw split 12"

CD & Vinyl available at Dusty Groove America, CD baby
Digital Releases at iTunes, Amazon, Wax Poetics Digital and more.
Retailers: request wholesale information from info@catune.com

www.catune.com

photo courtesy of the Joe Cuba estate

JOE CUBA

1931–2009

Fit to Be King

"I never wanted to be the king of boogaloo," Joe confessed to me a few years ago in his Spanish Harlem apartment. "I knew what was gonna happen. The minute boogaloo went out, the king would be out with it. Incidentally, I became the Father of Boogaloo. You know how I did that? I always stuck by my salsa."

Joe Cuba, or Sonny to those who knew him around the way, indeed stuck by his salsa and his hood. The two defined who he became, and throughout his life, he gave unconditionally to both. Aside from giving a generation of bilingual Puerto Ricans the boogaloo, Joe was the first to put congas on a stand ("I got them all standing, even Barretto"), introduced the vibes to Latin music ("If I had horns, the police would shut us down, so I used the vibes to keep the police from coming"), and he founded the Museum of La Salsa ("I wanted to show the world that Spanish Harlem made great cultural advancements and contributed to modern music"). When Joe died at the age of seventy-eight on February 15, 2008, Spanish Harlem lost one of its most soulful, passionate, and dedicated brothers.

Born Gilberto Miguel Calderón in 1931, Joe grew up on 116th Street in Spanish Harlem, the epicenter of modern Latin music. "Back then, Spanish Harlem was beautiful. Record shops lined 116th Street and constantly blasted music. A plate of rice and beans always waited for you around the corner. And we had stickball."

Stickball was Joe's first passion, but when he broke his leg in a pickup game, he found another talent while he waited for his cast to come off. A conga that helped him pass the time started his music career. "I would practice to Machito records when I wasn't outside on the stoop," Joe said. "There were a lot of musicians on my block. Santos Miranda and [Victor] 'Negrito' Pantoja lived close and motivated me."

In the early 1950s, after subbing for Sabu Martinez in La Alfarona X, Joe started his own group, Gilbert and the Cha Cha Boys. They hustled in clubs around Harlem, but it wasn't until promoter Catalino Rolón noticed them that they got some love. "[Catalino] got me a spot in the Stardust Ballroom," Joe said. "Before we went out, he asked me what the name of our band was, so I say, 'Gilbert and the Cha Cha Boys.' He says, 'You got to be kidding me! What kind of shit is that?' Later on that week, I'm reading the paper, and I see the ad for the Stardust Ballroom advertising this guy, Joe Cuba and his band. I get on the phone right away, all pissed, and I call up Catalino and say, 'Who's this asshole Joe Cuba?' Catalino says, 'That asshole is you!'"

With a new moniker, the Joe Cuba Sextet gradually made its mark on the Latin music scene playing mambo hits in English and Spanish. The band's bilingual versatility—thanks to crooners Cheo Feliciano, Nick Jimenez, and Jimmy Sabater—appealed to both Nuyoricans and White audiences, and soon Joe was performing side by side with heavyweights like Machito, Tito Puente, and Eddie Palmieri at the Palladium, the Plaza, and the Catskills Latin music circuit.

Joe's band exploded in the '60s with two jams that would provide the template for the boogaloo generation: "El Pito" and "Bang, Bang." Both tracks skillfully blended Latin montunos with grooving backbeats and soulful, bilingual lyrics; his music mirrored the mixed influences of his neighborhood. Though he birthed Latin soul, Joe always gave props to his hood. "I created the montuno, or the tune, but the audience created the boogaloo. Those two tunes came about because of the audience."

Like many of Spanish Harlem's successful musicians, Joe tried suburban life. But he couldn't stay away long. "A lot of people leave looking for their pot of gold, not realizing our pot of gold is right here," Joe said. "There are so many great things here in Harlem. A rich history, beautiful music, and great food." The music still blasts from the few remaining music shops on 116th Street, and rice and beans can still be grabbed on (almost) every corner. But it will be a little quieter, and a little sadder, without Spanish Harlem's proudest maestro-in-residence, Joe Cuba. ○ **Kristofer Ríos**

El Barrio

Latin Disco

Nuyorican sounds from the disco era

Featuring:
Louis Ramirez,
Charanga 76,
Tito Puente,
Joe Bataan,
Joe Cuba

Other titles in the El Barrio Series

  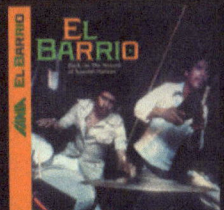 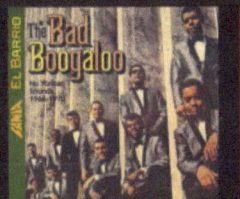 

To sign up for our new newsletter, and for downloads, news and more go to **www.fania.com**

RISING SONS
9dw proves seeds of funky fusion are best sown at home

Ask the leader of Japanese jazz-funk-fusion outfit 9dw who his biggest influences are, and he'll start with just one: his dad. "Music was always in the room in my childhood," says the multitalented Kensuke Saito, who plays guitars, keys, and synthesizers for the group. And the music in question was clearly some of the best. The Beatles, Billy Joel, Steely Dan, and Joe Sample are just a few that Saito lists, not to mention Michael Jackson, Prince, Genesis, and Mr. Mister, all of whom he first saw on the 1980s Japanese television program *Best Hit USA*. His father, however, remains the most important piece in Saito's musical biography, as he taught a thirteen-year-old Saito how to play guitar.

Now that he's grown, Saito continues to use the gifts of his father to make music with the Tokyo-based 9dw. The name stands for "Nine Days' Wonder," a proverb commonly associated with a brief sensation, something that swiftly enchants the public's imagination, only to disappear just as rapidly back into the depths of obscurity. When asked why he would choose to associate his band with the idea of a fleeting passion, Saito refers to the band's first 1997 incarnation, citing "the music we played at the time and the name matched."

More than a decade has passed since, and, after a few lineup changes, the group is now a four-piece consisting of Saito on lead guitar and keys, Masashi Kaneda on bass, Ryota Hayashida on synthesizers, and longtime friend Cozi Sato on drums. "We played together in [another] band fifteen years ago," Saito says of Sato. "I remember I met him for the first time in a record store in Shibuya, Tokyo." The tight-knit group keeps the process close to home with Saito writing and producing while Hayashida handles recording, mixing, and mastering. Saito stumbled upon the keyboard player while working in the studio in 2005. "It was the project of [another] band," recalls Saito. "He was there as a recording engineer." Two years down the line, the group began work on their debut album.

Laid down in the year between February '07 and '08, 9dw's self-titled album lands somewhere between the space-age vibe of Air's *Moon Safari* and the synth flexes of the Mackrosoft and Cheebacabra—with a solid influence of contemporary jazz from home. "Jazz, fusion, funk, electronic," says Saito, "it's hard to describe my music." With a sound as cohesive as it is expansive, they might be this era's answer to Marc Moulin's best work in Placebo, crafting futuristic instrumentals that are heavy on synthesizers, textured guitar work, relaxed breakbeats, and rhythmically engaging bass lines. Densely layered tracks like "Synthetic Avenues," "Black Coffee," or their first single, the up-tempo "Migrant," play like the robotic progeny of Herbie Hancock's fast-and-loose dates of the late '70s. The album is full of tightly constructed compositions, all of which were built on some serious vintage gear. A steady and rich analog sound flows from the Roland Juno-106, ARP Odyssey, Fender Jazz and Bottom Wave bass guitars, and Saito's own Fender Stratocaster. With both a nod to the 1970s and '80s and a lock on the hypermodern, 9dw are fast becoming the architects of twenty-first-century sonic daydreams worldwide. ○ **Jonathan Gelatt**

CHIN CHIN

THE FLASHING, THE FANCING
IN STORES AND ONLINE NOW

www.definitivejux.net
www.chinchin.tv
www.myspace.com/chinchinnyc

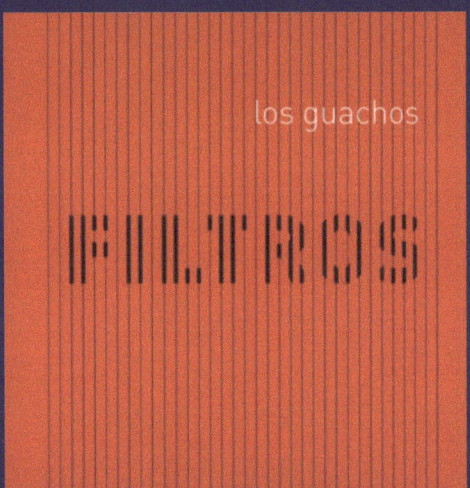

FILTROS by GUILLERMO KLEIN'S LOS GUACHOS
CD Album In Stores & iTunes on June 10

"Over the last 15 years or so, the pianist and composer Guillermo Klein has made a study of the tensile and elastic properties of rhythm. Along the way, he has built some fascinating bridges between jazz, pop, classical music and the chacareras and tangos of his native Argentina. His best music also carries smart harmonic ideas and surprising bolts of lyricism, but virtually all of it deals purposefully with the subject of groove."

—Nate Chinen **NY Times**

Guillermo will travel from his home in Barcelona for his annual gig with **Los Guachos** at *The Village Vanguard* during the week of June 10.

VIJAY IYER / TRAGICOMIC
CD Album In Stores & iTunes April 22

"One of the most important jazz pianists of his generation... The 'maximum creative risk' (that Vijay and his colleagues) are tackling is to make music that is not only brilliant, but relevant and democratic."

—Siddhartha Mitter **The Boston Globe**

On **Tragicomic** Iyer is accompanied by an amazing group of musicians: alto saxophonist Rudresh Mahanthappa, bassist Stephan Crump and drummer Marcus Gilmore.

Sunnyside

sunnysiderecords.com

photo by Peter Flutter

TIMELESS FREEDOM
Stonephace transcends the limitations of a genre

"I was very keen we made an album that was like something you'd turn up digging and couldn't quite work out when it was made, who made it, or what it was," explains producer Krzysztof Oktalski, half the brains behind Stonephace. Seamlessly shifting through genres, Stonephace is the creation of Oktalski and jazz veteran Larry Stabbins, two acclaimed artists that, despite their backgrounds, have formed a complementary relationship. Pulling sounds off the shelf, Stonephace is both rooted in the sounds of the past, while looking toward the future. "For a moment, I could pretend to be Pharoah Sanders or Junior Walker or Mike Ratledge," admits saxophonist Stabbins. "I suppose it uses the cut-and-paste ethics of hip-hop and the references to the past but without sampling."

Meeting in Cornwall, Stabbins and Oktalski were drawn to each other regardless of their separate musical paths and genres. "I've always liked outsider music," says Stabbins. "Despite my background, I very often find working with people who don't have the traditional musical background and education far more interesting and creative." A veteran of the European free-jazz and improvisational communities, Stabbins first came to prominence in the '70s working with pianist Keith Tippett in the jazz/prog-rock orchestra Centipede. From there, Stabbins went on to collaborate with Simon Booth in the pop groups Weekend and Working Week, along with also forming QRZ?, a jazz/rap group.

"It's hard to find collaborators you share perspective with here [in Cornwall]," says Oktalski. Known for his work as one of the leading DJs in the Cornish rave scene, Oktalski formed a bond with Stabbins that has allowed the two to work off each other and create the groove-centered, psychedelic sounds of Stonephace. "We have entirely complementary skills—everything I'm really bad at, Krzysztof is really good at, and vice versa," explains Stabbins.

Initially a duo, Stabbins and Oktalski began recording together simply for the pleasure of making music, with Oktalski programming and Stabbins blaring his sax over what he heard. "The wonderful thing about this album to me is the way it's just grown organically almost from nowhere and with no expectations," says Stabbins. "And people have got involved simply because they liked the music." After playing some of the tracks for Portishead guitarist Adrian Utley, musicians from Stabbins's past began to add their pieces to the mix. Utley, whom Stabbins first met in the late '80s, immediately expressed interest in playing on the album and laid down tracks right away, many of which were first takes. From there, Utley suggested another old friend, bassist Jim Barr. Also in the mix is legendary trumpeter Guy Barker, with whom Stabbins worked in the '70s London jazz scene. For live shows, keyboardist Helm DeVegas makes an appearance along with visuals from Stella Marina.

"Producers from a DJing background often seem to spend their lives yearning for the expression and creative freedom of jazz; similarly, jazz musicians tire of aging audiences, the consistency of their sonic palette, and the limitations of the genre," admits Oktalski. "We started from those positions a long time ago, but along the way we've transcended it by absorbing so much from each other." ○ **Chris Arena**

THE BEST OF RAY CAMACHO & THE TEARDROPS

A killer 16 track compilation featuring Ray's blend of **Chicano Salsa, Funk Cumbia** and **Soul** from 1968-1971. Compiled by **Pete Issac** of **Jelly Jazz**.
CD/45

THE FANTASTICS! - MIGHTY RIGHTEOUS

A fresh, 21st century take on the soul-jazz, blues and funk template includes the hit 45 **'Soul Child'** featuring **Noel Mckoy**.
CD/LP/45

DJ GRAHAM B - NO ROOM FOR CHAIRS

DJ Graham B blends brazilian beats, funky organ loops, ska and latin sounds for all hip dancefloors.
CD

NATHAN HAINES - RIGHT NOW

Respected saxman / producer features the vocals of **Marlena Shaw, Ty** and **Vanessa Freeman** mixing soul, RnB, soulful house and jazz.
CD/12

DJ LUBI PRESENTS SALSA DURA!

The famed DJ selects some of the hottest, hardest salsa tracks from around the world including **Jimmy Bosch, Santiago All Stars** and **Snowboy**.
CD/12/45

THE APPLES - THE POWER 12
Genre busting band cover **Snap** & **Rage Against the Machine**.

FREESTYLE
www.freestylerecords.co.uk
www.myspace.com/freestylerecordsuk

M9 RECORDINGS PRESENT:

MAGIC HEART GENIES

NEW ALBUM "HEARTIFACT" AVAILABLE ON ITUNES

"Double-time super-rapping meets soulful production for an understated masterpiece"
- Toph One, XLR8R, Dec. 08

12" & CDs AVAILABLE!

Check out our website for free downloads and more info about our project at:

WWW.MAGICHEARTGENIES.COM

Rite of Passage

The making of *Ululation* was a celebration of life

text **Seb Carayol**

A Visual Sound isn't your average skateboard flick. Put out by Stereo Skateboards in 1994 to promote its team's exploits, its aesthetics were definitely different. *A Visual Sound*'s non-skate interludes, largely filmed by Stereo co-owner-turned-actor Jason Lee in Super 8, gave it a definitely incongruous visual identity. A true experimental journey in a world then governed by tasteless *über*-baggy, orange pants courtesy of now-defunct brands such as Fuct or Droors. But what's been the most intriguing thing about *A Visual Sound* in skate-nerd circles for the past fifteen years is its soundtrack. Out of the nine tunes backing jazzy skateboarding by the likes of Ethan Fowler, Carl Shipman, Jason Lee, and company, seven came from one single Coltrane-inspired jazz album, mysteriously titled *Ululation*. Only available by calling a phone number in New York, the closing credits stated. And that was it. In 2009, the number is long gone, and so seemed *Ululation* with its oddly named tracks: "Borderline Case," "Blue Barracudas," "Utensil," "Hunca Munca."

It was time to do something.

Chris Pastras, the current co-owner of Stereo, should know more about the affair. After all, this accomplished artist obsessed with a certain idea of retro Americana is the one who chose this album for his video, taking the risk to end years of Daisy Age hip-hop/Beastie Boys/Bad Religion supremacy in skate flicks. "I got the cassette from a friend in New York," he explains. "Her dad played on it, and I thought it sounded just rad." Other details are hazy, and, yes, Pastras lost contact long ago. Seems like a borderline case of giving up is on its way… That is, until the stars aligned in one of these particularly coincidental moments.

One week after this conversation with Pastras, and after a fifteen-year-long search, a nostalgic, over-the-hill skateboarder known as yours truly scored a copy of the *Ululation* LP out of the clear blue sky. At last. Enough to howl at the moon like the wolf that adorns its cover.

With the album credits in hand, the real quest could now begin. As sensed from the elusiveness of this 1987 release, the six-track LP had an amazing story to tell. Especially the musicians playing on it.

Valery Ponomarev is one of them.[1] After he fled Russia in 1971, making his way to New York in '73, the trumpet player replaced Bill Hardman in Art Blakey's Jazz Messengers from 1977 to 1979, and recorded nine albums. He's played since on dozens of records and still leads his own big band. Yet, the *Ululation* sessions stand out as a particular souvenir for this jazz legend. "I remember very well," he enthusiastically recalls on the phone. "My friend Jeff Hittman called me one day to go do this rehearsal. This guy John Krasnow wanted to put an album together; he played baritone sax, but he wasn't a professional musician. So we went, and we started rehearsing. And with all due respect, there wasn't much to rehearse except that we kept rehearsing and getting together and getting paid for all this time. And the record ended up sounding fantastic."

True, John Lee Krasnow, who passed away in 1991, wasn't a musician by trade. But by heart, definitely. Raised in Closter, New Jersey, he fell in love with music after fourth grade, as he explained in a 1989 radio interview: "I wound up looking up instruments in the dictionary, and next to each instrument was a little picture. And only because I liked the little picture of the clarinet, I decided to play clarinet. Saxophone interest came up later, when I started listening to the

rock, doo-wop, and rhythm and blues groups of the '50s."[2] Eventually, his taste for music landed him a spot as one of Columbia Records marketing heads, where he worked when the *Ululation* sessions took place.

"What's the most interesting is the recording itself," says Ponomarev, who was perplexed by the sessions. "All the guys were continually high from I don't know what plus alcohol; they went nuts. It was continuous anecdotes, continuous laughs. It was going on and on. Couple guys got so high, it got almost intolerable." Janice Friedman, the pianist, was equally struck by the strange, festive, decadent mayhem. "Everyone came over to my home maybe once a week to practice for quite a while," she says. "I have a nice piano and a drum set, so it was an easy place to hang. It was a big party really, and we practiced his tunes, ate, tipped a few. It was quite a ball, and along the way, we learned the music. John [Krasnow] seemed a bit uncomfortable, because I don't think he really knew most of the folks in the band." She stops briefly. And hands the key to unlock the *Ululation* mystery: "We didn't realize that the party was part of John's parting plans."

Because there was one more thing that John Krasnow forgot to tell the musicians: he was terminally ill. And he knew it. "He contracted [type 1] diabetes in 1988," one of his two daughters, Highlyann, now thirty-two and residing in Brooklyn, discloses. "It was very difficult to control, and he had a very rough time until he died in 1991, after contracting meningitis."

Upon Krasnow's death, about four years after *Ululation* was released, the oddity of its sessions made perfect sense. "Only when he passed, I could kind of see why they were acting the way they did," Ponomarev recalls. "And I understood why John's father was there and was putting up the money for the recording: so John's music would exist after his death. His family knew; we didn't. I'm sure the guys would have acted differently if they knew what was going on. Only *then* I understood why John *needed* to have his music recorded so fast. Krasnow was a beautiful person, and it was very upsetting to know that he was gone." A few years later, ace alto saxophonist Jeff Hittman died as well.

Even so, twenty years have gone and death still loses the battle: *Ululation* is a jazzy ode to a vibrant, untamed life. "A brilliant album, really," Ponomorev says triumphantly. A pretty funny one too, as its definite melancholy is always balanced by a note of dark humor. "I remember laughing about the titles of the tunes," Friedman giggles, "not really understanding the meaning for him until later. [The unreleased] 'Song Without Mayo,' for example." The best part being when Krasnow came up with his own sweet and sour explanations. Exhibit A, his 1989 radio interview, when asked where his inspiration came from: "That's a good question. And I haven't come up with a really good answer, but I do have an interesting story. I actually read in a magazine that some scientist figured out that if you breathe through your left nostril, you will stimulate the right side, or the imaginative/creative side of the brain. So one morning I sat down, and I breathed through my left nostril for about fifteen minutes—he said it has to be about ten or fifteen minutes. I'm glad no one else was around, and all I can say is it didn't seem to work. Other than that, I don't know how I do get my ideas. They just seem to pop into my head, perhaps they percolate in the subconscious."[3]

No matter what inner circuitry they followed, *Ululation*'s six tracks ended up being ready to go. As were at least seven other tracks for a future *Ululation 2*, completed in 1991 right before Krasnow died, which never saw the light of day—yet. Once the unconventional artwork was completed, with its howling wolf in primary colors (perhaps a swan song allegory? Krasnow never really divulged the reason), the album was ready to ship. But no record company went ahead with the project. Columbia, where Krasnow worked, generously accepted to offer it with the Columbia Records and Tape Club catalog for each new member, but that was about it.

John Krasnow was alone. He proceeded to start his own label, Long Shot Records, and pressed a few hundred copies, "not more than about one thousand," his daughter Highlyann states. *Ululation* got exclusively sold mail-order-style from his home. And that could have been it. But Highlyann passed a tape to the right person in 1994. Namely, Gio Estevez, an influential artist for the New York City skateboarding scene, and a good friend of Stereo Skateboards owner Chris Pastras. Seven years after its initial release, *Ululation* became *A Visual Sound*'s soundtrack[4] and one of skateboarding's cult classics. A surprise that even the facetious John Krasnow probably hadn't planned. ⬤

Wax Poetics Records will be releasing *Ululation* and *Ululation 2* on vinyl and digitally.

Notes

1. Full personnel, as credited on the LP: Valery Ponomarev (trumpet), Jeff Hittman (alto sax), Jerry Vejmola (tenor sax), John Lee Krasnow (baritone sax), Janice Friedman (piano), Bill Patton (bass), Yoshitaka Uematsu (drums).
2. The full 1989 Krasnow interview, from Bergen Community College's program *This Is Bergen*, can be heard here: www.bergen.edu/faculty/mkatzman/Bulldog%20Radio01.mp3
3. Ibid
4. For the first time since 1994, Stereo Skateboards has just released *A Visual Sound* on DVD. Check www.stereosoundagency.com for info.

THE SCION tC

Stand together by standing apart. Make your mark on the Scion tC.

Vehicles shown are special project cars, modified with non-Genuine Scion parts and accessories. Modification with these non-Genuine Scion parts or accessories will void the Scion warranty, may negatively impact vehicle performance & safety, and may not be street legal. For more information, call 866-70-SCION (866-707-2466) or visit Scion.com. © 2009 Scion, a marque of Toyota Motor Sales, U.S.A., Inc. All rights reserved. Scion, the Scion logo, and tC are trademarks of Toyota Motor Corporation.

what moves you

ENGINE OF CHANGE

Guitarist Melvin Sparks fueled funky sessions for soul-jazz's master mechanics

text **Bill Carbone**

An unfailingly humble man, Melvin Sparks seems to locate himself on the fringes of jazz history. Though he glows while recounting memorable incidents from his forty years in jazz—especially when the story calls for a Lou Donaldson or Jack McDuff impression—Sparks is just as likely to speak like a fan, fawning over Sonny Stitt's chops or Oliver Nelson's arrangements, or even confessing that he was nearly overcome with nerves upon finally sharing the stage with Jimmy Cobb in 2008.

It would be easy enough to allow Sparks to slip through the cracks; of the hundred-some albums on which he performed, only eleven were as a leader, and most of those are currently out of print. Moreover, while several of his contemporaries are now international marquee names in jazz, Sparks works sporadically and mostly in the Northeast. Yet this would be overlooking Sparks's subtle but important contribution to soul jazz in the late '60s and early '70s. Musicians a generation older than Sparks—Stitt, Donaldson, McDuff—hired him because he could hang with the tempos and harmonic sophistication of their older repertoire, but also for the funky chicken-scratch rhythm guitar that kept their music fresh and current. In short, Sparks brought the funk.

Like many Southern musicians at the time, Sparks worked his way into the music industry via R&B. Still a teenager, he departed his Houston, Texas, home first as a member of the Upsetters, then the backing band for soul revues with headliners such as Sam Cooke, Johnnie Taylor, and Little Richard (he shared a bus bench with the young Jimi Hendrix). In 1965, Sparks left the Upsetters with hopes of launching a jazz career. "I thought I was just going to show up and start my band and 'upset' New York with it," Sparks recalls, "[but] an older guy at a session pulled me aside and told me it wasn't going to be like that. He said, 'You're not ready; you've got to get you a job with somebody older and learn.' Then the Upsetters called and asked me to go back on the road, and I went."

However, events unfolded more as he had originally envisioned when Sparks returned to New York in late 1966. As he tells it, Sparks befriended both George Benson and his idol Grant Green within his first few days of arriving. Moreover, Benson quickly began siphoning his runoff gigs to Sparks, the best of which was his recently vacated spot in Jack McDuff's quartet. Sparks was in.

Over roughly the next fifteen years, Sparks recorded several solo albums and appeared on numerous others with McDuff, Lou Donaldson, Sonny Stitt, Lonnie Smith, Charles Earland, Idris Muhammad, Reuben Wilson, Rusty Bryant, Leon Spencer, and Charles Kynard. Many of the sides he recorded—Donaldson's "Hot Dog," "It's Your Thing," and "Everything I Do Gohn Be Funky (From Now On)," Wilson's "Bus Ride" and "Orange Peel," and Earland's "Black Talk" to name a few—are genre-defining tracks performed and sampled countless times since.

Though he continued to record throughout the '80s, cutting sides with Hank Crawford, Jimmy McGriff, Houston Person, and Johnny Lytle, among others, Sparks earned his living primarily as the leader of a wedding band. However, like many soul-jazz musicians from his generation, he was inspired to go public again in the '90s after being alerted to samples of his guitar on everything from Brand Nubian to Madlib, and by groups like the Greyboy Allstars performing his music on the jam-band scene. Since then, Sparks has been a featured guest with several jam bands, released five solo albums, and toured internationally, this time performing to a mostly White audience roughly his children's age.

I first met Melvin as a journalist, but soon after I also began playing drums in his band. Our occasional road trips are, for me, equal parts gigging and history lesson. This excerpted interview was conducted over the course of two, two-hour car rides in which I played tracks from Melvin's oeuvre as well as songs in which a sample of his guitar figures prominently, asked questions about them, and just let the music roll to see what happened.

Illustration by Josh Dunn.

"Duffin' Around"
Jack McDuff & David Newman *Double Barrelled Soul* (Atlantic) 1968

Who is this, Karl Denson?

No! It's Jack McDuff, *Double Barreled Soul*. This is one of your first sessions in New York, right?

Yes, it's not my first though.

Did those guys ride you on your playing; was it an educational thing?

No, they were relying on me because of my youth, my age, and to get the feel of the "today's experience." McDuff was from an old school; they were from the '50s, and I'm from the mid-'60s and '70s, coming out of the Upsetters. So McDuff would write me a song and call a rehearsal, and then he would take all his rhythm ideas from me. He'd say, "Okay, Melvin, what do you think, let's play it this way." And sometimes I'd say, "Oh no, McDuff, let's play here, let's try this," and McDuff would give it some thought, and often times he would go with the rhythm I'd recommend. Not all the time, but most of the time.

"Son of Ice Bag"
Lonnie Smith *Think!* (Blue Note) 1968

[*Sparks begins laughing immediately*]
You recognize this one.

Oh yeah! It's easy for me to remember that, because that's my arrangement. This is a Hugh Masekela tune called "Son of Ice Bag," and actually McDuff was going to cover it, and I liked the idea so much that I used a portion of McDuff's idea and wrote this out for Lonnie Smith's record. Lonnie doesn't read music, so we had to rehearse it a few times before David ["Fathead"] Newman and Lee Morgan [came in]. They just read it right at the record date.

Did you know those guys already?

I knew Fathead, but I didn't know Lee that well. When Lee found out he was doing a record with Lonnie, he sent word out through the producers that he wasn't gonna be in no studio with guys humming parts to him and singing and all of that stuff, you know; he wanted charts. Now that I look back on it, I think Lee wanted to do the charts to get paid for it! So that got back to Lonnie, and Lonnie told me about it, and I wrote out all the charts.

"More Today Than Yesterday"
Charles Earland *Black Talk!* (Prestige) 1970

This was a *huge* hit; this was the record that put me on the map. It was one of the few, during those days, that hit in the so-called Black market, and because of the song, it actually crossed over [to a White audience] a little bit. The [original] song was very popular, and what Charles did to it was…actually all he did was put a Lou Donaldson groove on it!

Believe it or not, this was either a second- or third-take version; we didn't spend a lot of time on this song, because it was written out. That's why if you listen to it closely, the ending is messed up. We never got the ending right, they just kept it; they didn't want to do it again.

Were these pop songs an important part of what you were doing then as far as having a hook for people?

No, what happened was, basically, looking back on it, when I first came to New York, it was like the older guys would play standards, which is just another word for "cover." Charlie Parker didn't write those songs, those were standards that they had to play and then create a performance on. Well, the R&B music that the jazz musicians were covering was the same idea, because a lot of those songs became the standards of that day—like "More Today Than Yesterday," [and] Ramsey Lewis covered "The 'In' Crowd." All those kinds of songs and the James Brown songs were being covered by jazz musicians.

"Turn It On!"
Sonny Stitt *Turn It On!* (Prestige) 1971

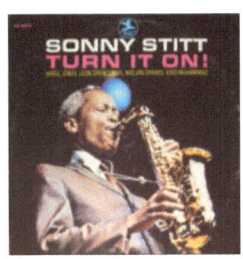

[*Sparks laughs immediately; he clearly loves to hear this track*]
That's Sonny Stitt. Leon Spencer, "Turn It On." This is a great tune, man! Leon wrote all of the stuff for that record.

So was Sonny Stitt reaching out to you guys to harness the new young sound?
No, this was done by the producer, Bob Porter. Porter went to Sonny and asked him, "Why should Lou Donaldson make all the money?"

So was Sonny into it?
Yeah! Sonny was like, "Okay, let's go in and do it." Leon was the first organ player to play like this. He was throwing everybody a curve, because wasn't nobody supposed to play the organ—I'm talkin' about the bass now—wasn't nobody supposed to play the bass like that on the organ. You were supposed to be just walkin' straight, playing straight on the beat stuff. Leon was trying to play like a bass player.

Did you guys gig with Sonny at all?
I did, not Leon. [But Stitt] just made the record; he didn't want to do it live. [At concerts] he had me in there playing that bebop. That's why I play so much bebop now, because of guys like him and Lou. When Sonny plays…I was like, *man*! [*sings along with Stitt's solo, laughing*] Sonny Stitt was the baddest—that cat was something else, man. And check out me and Leon! And Idris! We're just going crazy on this thing, man! We had some moments on this tune! That was some great stuff there, brother!

"Whip! Whop!"
Melvin Sparks *Texas Twister* (Eastbound) 1973

Uh-oh! Karl [Denson] and them—Greyboy Allstars—man, they love this song.

Did you do the arrangement?
I wrote all this stuff out. I wrote the song. Even what the bass player is playing, all that is written out.

How did you compose, piano?
I don't use any instrument, man.

Straight from your head to paper?
Yep.

Were you able to try out some of this stuff before the session?
No, because I came to New York as an arranger. When I was on the road with the Upsetters, I was the musical coordinator; I did all the arranging for that band. So when I got to New York, I knew enough about arranging that when I wrote something, I already knew what it sounded like; I didn't need to rehearse.

"Get Down with the Get Down"
Melvin Sparks '75 (Westbound) 1975

Melvin Sparks '75! The piano player and organ player on this record is Earl Van Dyke. He was one of the founding members of the Funk Brothers at Motown.

That's interesting because I was thinking that this heads in a different direction. On "Whip! Whop!" you're moving towards a funk thing, but this one, it's *funk*.

Now these arrangements I did not write, these are all Motown guys on here. What happened was that the record company [Westbound] owner wanted to put me in a more popular bag. So he put all these horns on there. They wanted me to be funk—jazz but funky. But the producer on this, for this record company, was…. Okay, this is the literal truth: he was a five-hundred-pound gay man who liked me. I was skinny in those days. And, in those days, I was also with the so-called quote-unquote "Black Muslims." And when he found out I was a Black Muslim, he hated me for that. He even tried to ruin this record.

The record company, after Melvin Sparks '75, they started another record on me on which they had Funkadelic-Parliament to lay the tracks. And this guy tried his last-ditch effort to have a relationship with me. He said, "Melvin, I want you to come up to the hotel. I want you to listen to these tracks to see what you think. We want you to go to the studios and *blah blah blah*." So I get up to the hotel, and he tells me, "Yeah, Melvin, c'mon in, man," and starts playing the music. He says, "Man, take off your shoes," and "Relax, man, take off your shirt, take off your clothes." That's when I said, "Man, look, I do not do any kind of sexual thing with another man. I will not do that, I flatly refuse that." And I told him point-blank like that!

It's wild that he didn't figure that out ahead of time.

Well, he knew, but he was making his pitch; he figured he could break me, especially when he got George Clinton and those guys to do those tracks. I wasn't in the studio when they done those tracks. They were some dynamite tracks, man.

And you never got to play on them.

I got to play on them, but he messed it all up.

So they never got released?

No, they never got finished. And now, the company's totally into gospel, and that guy's dead. I saw Bernie Worrell and asked if he remembered the tracks, but he doesn't. The people on the tracks, they had one bass player called P-Nut, the other was Bootsy. Then they had Bernie, and Gary Shider playing guitar on there. But, man, that stuff was some smoking tracks! I woulda been a big star if those tracks had hit. I tell you, man, that was some smoking stuff!

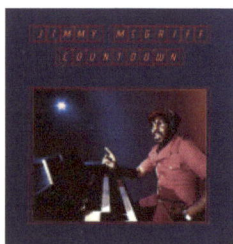

"I'm Walking"
Jimmy McGriff *Countdown* (Milestone) 1983

Oh, Fats Domino, I was the one who told McGriff to play this tune, to learn it for the recording session.

You ran in the same circle with Jimmy McGriff for a long time, but I don't think you recorded with him until the '80s.

I never was in his band; I always substituted for his guitar player. But he started using me as a producer. Bob Porter told him he should use me. And after the first record I did, he started using me on almost everything. Jimmy really gave me some opportunities when I was making those records. He let me bring songs and arrange songs right on the spot.

And he would listen to what I say, he'd say, "Sparks, what are you talking about, man? Show me what you're talking about." So I'd go to the organ and give him an idea what I was talking about. Can you imagine me going to the organ giving Jimmy McGriff something? But that's what he asked me to do.

He was something else, man. He was kind of hard to play with as a guitar player. Even [as] a drummer.

Why was that?

'Cause you never knew what he was going to do, never. He never played a song the same way; you'd never know what he was playing. After he started playing it, you'd say, "Oh, he's playing 'I Got a Woman,'" but you'd be a minute into the song before you knew it. He never said nothing. I mean, I did a couple of three-month runs with him, and I tell you, man, night after night, it was the same thing. It was hard to play with Jimmy. You never knew what key he was playing in. Sometimes, he'd come out of E-flat and go to D-flat and play a song in D-flat, and then you'd end up in B-flat.

And you just had to listen for that?

You could listen all you want, but you'd be fiddlin' around trying to figure it out. Because there wasn't an arrangement, you just had to follow the best you could. You had to open up your ears; you had to have big ears to play with him. Lou Donaldson used to do that, but at least when Lou would start a tune, you knew what it was, at least you could follow him, and after a couple of choruses, you'd probably have it. Not with Jimmy, ooh-wee! But when it comes to a groove, nobody's better.

Would those guys mix in new tunes every night or did you play the same set?

They didn't have no set list! They just play, man. You go to the gig and play—that was it. If you were a good musician, you could get over; if you weren't, you'd embarrass yourself, because they'd sure enough embarrass you. I mean, they would let you embarrass yourself; they wouldn't stop you from doing that.

"Donkey Walk"
Lou Donaldson *Everything I Play Is Funky* (Blue Note) 1969

Oh ho ho, Papa Lou!

This is one of those songs where Lou had to calm me down. I wanted to play so much stuff on this. [*imitates Donaldson in a high voice*] "Nah, man, just take it easy, don't play all that shit." That's the way they talked. "You can't play all that, man, just play the blues, man." I was the only one Lou had to tell that to; everybody else was fine. I was like, "Man, I'm gonna play all this George Benson stuff! I'm gonna tear this song up!" I learned so much stuff from Lou Donaldson; that's when I stopped trying to play like George and started to play like Melvin Sparks.

Is this Lou's tune?

Yep. [Lou's] daughter was going to University of Chicago, and he was trying to make hit after hit after hit; that's all that was on his mind. Because he had to pay for that education; that stuff was killin' him! He did it though.

"3 in the Head"
Run-DMC *Down with the King* (Arista) 1993

What is this, Madlib?

Do you hear that sample that it's built on?

Who is that, Idris and Charlie Earland?

Yeah, that's "Donkey Walk," just slowed down.

Right!

So if you just heard that, would you have picked up on that being a tune you were on?

No, but there was a guy that sent me a tape. He had—I think it was twenty-eight samples of me—he had all of it.

So, what do you think about sampling?

Well, I love it; it's kind of what brought me back from the dead. The only thing I don't like about it is that as a sideman I never got paid for any of this stuff. And I feel that I should be paid as a session for each one of those samples. Not royalties, but as if I was there doing a recording session. Lou would collect for this because he was the songwriter. They used my version of "It's Your Thing" from a Lou record, but Lou didn't get paid for that, the Isley Brothers did. And I thought that was wrong. But they have to pay royalties to someone; I don't know how that works. Anyway, we didn't get paid, me and Idris, Charles Earland, we didn't get a dime. We didn't even get recognized. As far as I know, our name doesn't show up on any of their material written, you know. Sean Combs, who knows my daughters and everything, never said a word about me, but he knew who I was, he sampled my music—he sampled it for Biggie Smalls, you know, and never said a word. [*chuckles*]

So have any of the guys from this newer generation ever gotten in touch with you?

No.

But you think that the sampling helped start your career back up?

Well, between that and Jerry Garcia and them kind of people, you know.

What's the Jerry Garcia thing, the jam-band community?

Well, yeah, because he knew about, he knew about those records. That's what they were imitating when he did…what's the organ player we were talking about earlier?

Merl Saunders.

Merl. When they did that stuff, that's where they was getting it from. I always wondered how those kind of guys knew me, Bob Weir and all them guys were like, "Oh, you Melvin Sparks, I heard about you." I appreciate Jerry Garcia for that.

"I'd Rather Be Your Lover"
Madonna *Bedtime Stories* (Sire) 1994

Oh, I know this.

"It's Your Thing."

Yeah, Lou Donaldson.

Have you heard this? It's Madonna. You're on a Madonna track!

No! [*Laughing*] Well, this is the third track that this was used on that I've heard. De La Soul did it, and then I think some Jamaican group or something did it. Oh, that's really something.

 I remember one time, man, I was home looking at TV, watching the Martin Lawrence show, and at the end, who pops up there but a sample of me playing and Martin trying to rap on it. I, like, fell through the floor! I was like, "Ahh, man! Oh boy!" ◐

Bill Carbone is working towards his PhD in ethnomusicology at Wesleyan University and is also an active musician. He can be reached at myspace.com/billcarbone.

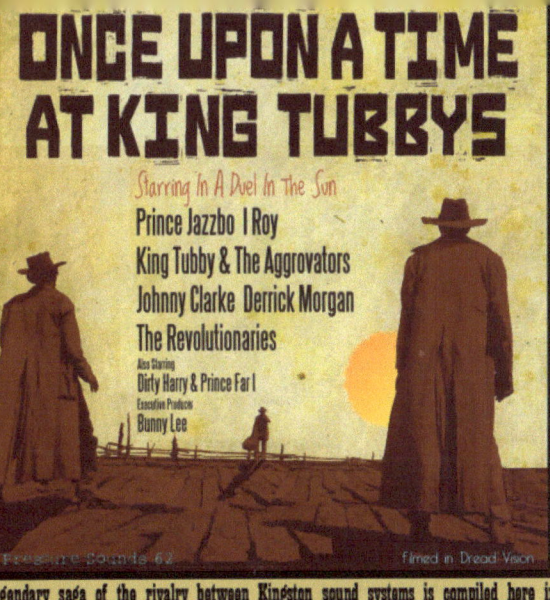

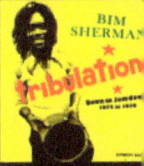

EASY STAR ALL-STARS

EASY STAR'S LONELY HEARTS DUB BAND

A REGGAE RE-IMAGINING OF THE BEATLES' SGT. PEPPER'S LONELY HEARTS CLUB BAND
FROM THE BAND BEHIND DUB SIDE OF THE MOON & RADIODREAD

WITH A LITTLE HELP FROM THEIR FRIENDS...
STEEL PULSE • MATISYAHU • MICHAEL ROSE • U ROY
BUNNY RUGS • LUCIANO • RANKING ROGER • MAX ROMEO
SUGAR MINOTT • FRANKIE PAUL • MIGHTY DIAMONDS

IN STORES APRIL 14, 2009

Safe Haven

Pianist and composer Horace Tapscott cultivated the Los Angeles jazz community

text **Andy Thomas**

"I am Horace Tapscott
My fingers are dancing grassroots
I do not fit into form, I create form
My ears are radar charting the whispers of my ancestors
I seek the divinity in outcasts, the richness of rebels"

–Kamau Daaood, from the poem "PAPA, the Lean Griot"

"It's like bringing up your children in a certain area because you want them to grow and be aware of certain things. This same principle applied to us, as far as Black musicians were concerned," proclaimed the late pianist, composer, teacher, and community activist Horace Tapscott in the notes to *Live at I.U.C.C.* by the Pan Afrikan Peoples Arkestra, the towering spiritual jazz ensemble founded by Tapscott in his adopted home of Los Angeles back in 1961.

Formed as a self-help arts collective to bring pride to the community, the Arkestra symbolized Tapscott's desire for Black empowerment, and the need for his people to reach back to their ancestral roots for survival. Over thirty years and amid two major social uprisings, the musical and social guidance of this modern-day urban griot helped create a sense of family and belonging across the generations, as an artistic village was built within Los Angeles's socially divided sprawl.

Born in 1934, Horace Tapscott spent his early years in Houston, where he soon became acutely aware of the chains that bound him. "When we got on the bus, my mother started heading right to the back of the bus by the 'Colored' sign," he recalled to political writer Michael Slate shortly before his death in 1999. "And I remember my mother saying, 'Come here, Horace.' And I said I wanted to sit where I was."

Arriving in California in 1943, Horace's mother headed straight for the jazz hub of Central Avenue, introducing her son to the cats hanging around the Black Musicians' Union. At the age of fourteen, Horace met Cecilia, who became his soul mate and eventually his wife. "Cecilia and I used to walk

The Arkestra in performance at the IUCC, circa late 1970s/early 1980s. Photo by Mark Weber.

the streets together, and we got to see all these people," he recalled in his autobiography, *Songs of the Unsung*. "We used to listen to Art Tatum, Red Callender, and Bill Douglass." He was soon playing trombone alongside the likes of Dexter Gordon and Eric Dolphy, and started to appreciate the importance of togetherness and the role of culture in social advancement. "It had to do with a feeling and a hookup to creativity and understanding," continued Horace, "and how people can come together regardless of what's happening around them." These creative interactions opened up a whole world of collaboration and cooperation to the inquisitive young musician, who would use these experiences as the foundation for his own jazz collective.

After a stint in the Air Force in the mid-'50s, which, he recalled, "got me ready to come out into the world," Horace went on tour with Lionel Hampton, switching to the piano and eventually becoming disillusioned with the showmanship of the band. "I wanted to do something else," he wrote in his autobiography. "I wanted my own thing; I wanted to write it and help preserve the music."

Returning to South Central in the early '60s, Horace found an area blighted by years of neglect and direct racial attacks by Chief William H. Parker's LAPD. As social deprivation grew in relation to the "proactive policing" and what many saw as the deliberate destruction of the African American community, an alterative support structure was desperately needed. The Pan Afrikan Peoples Arkestra (also known as the Underground Musicians Association or UGMA) was formed by Tapscott in 1961 under the maxim: "Our music is contributive rather than competitive." Whether loading instruments onto flatbed trucks to play on street corners, holding sessions at old folks' homes, hospitals, and prisons, or teaching music and poetry in elementary schools, the Ark's members set out on their mission to preserve the arts in the Black community by taking the music to the people.

The cultural and social experimentation of Tapscott's radical arts group anticipated the later work of better-known jazz collectives like the St. Louis–based Black Artists Group and Chicago's Association for the Advancement of Creative Musicians, and matched the powerful collective energy of Sun Ra's better-known Arkestra. "Of course I was aware of Sun Ra's Arkestra, always respected what he was doing, and got my spelling of that word from him, but that was as far as the hookup went," Tapscott recalled. "While he was thinking in terms of space, of an ark traveling through space, I was thinking in terms of a cultural safe house for the music."

Central to the growth of the Ark was its family ethos and reaching out to the children in order to continue the lineage. At the heart of the family was the organization's matriarch, Linda Hill, who not only helped balance some of the macho weight that was thrown around but also provided the group's first home, which was celebrated by Horace in one of the Ark's standards, "Lino's Pad." In Steve Isoardi's book *The Dark Tree*, another sister, trumpeter Danyel Romero, recalled the deep contribution Hill made to the Ark: "Linda was like a big flower… She was connected to the spirits or sources of the unseen world that most of us were not dealing with." While Linda certainly became an important figure for women in the organization, Elaine Brown, Black Panther activist and close friend of the bandleader, also found in Horace a man who was equally at home in women's company. "He was the most non-egocentric man you could imagine and a real friend to us as women," she says fondly. "He didn't have that macho thing but was very protective and was a man in every sense of the word."

While a family was most definitely being developed at Linda's place, it was not one based on any traditional American model, with the mysticism and bohemian atmosphere enhanced by the constant use of herb. "We were just wild," recalls saxophonist Arthur Blythe. "It was like we were part of that hippie movement, but we were like Black hippies. It was experience with drugs, music, freedom." Elaine Brown certainly concurs with this image for the man who later became known as "the Phantom" because of his late-night drop-ins on friends. "Horace smoked weed all the time," she laughs affectionately, "and I mean all the time."

By the mid-'60s, the Ark had become a powerful vessel, sending positive vibrations right across South Central L.A. In *Songs of the Unsung*, Tapscott recalled how he sought out freethinking band members who might bring something new to the Ark: "I started by looking for different kinds of personalities who were involved in the music. And every person I brought in was an outsider, so to speak." One of those outsiders was a young conguero named Taumbu, who rode with the Ark throughout the '60s. "I was living in Venice Beach when I was invited to the UGMA house," Taumbu recalls. "It was [a place] for real resistance artists. At the time, I was a fugitive of the L.A. police. Also, I was homeless… It was about Blackness and Black music without compromise."

Alongside the dedication to the family was an even stronger commitment to defend the community at

(top) Horace Tapscott and Arthur Blythe, 1980. (bottom left) Nimbus recording session fo Billie Harris's *I Want Some Water*, 1983. Billie, soprano sax; Horace Tapscott, piano. (bottom right) Horace Tapscott and Cecil Taylor, circa 1979 Photos by Mark Weber.

Horace Tapscott and Will Connell at Will's house, 1970. Photo by Michael Dett Wilcots.

large. "It was a revolutionary period, and all the cats and chicks were revolutionaries in the true sense of the word," Taumbu explains. Invoking the mantra of the great Fela Ransome-Kuti, the Arkestra trombonist Lester Robertson proclaimed, "This horn is a weapon, and I'm prepared to use it like that."

This was a time of some serious thinking in the Black community. "I got exposed to Elijah Muhammad, Malcolm, and Dr. King," Horace told Steve Isoardi. "There were certain Black men out there who seemed to be working for the betterment of the whole country. We were feeling that if we were together, we'd be an asset to our environment." In "dashikis and them long naturals," the group spoke to their people with a stark, direct truth. "We were also talking against the things that were happening in the community, like police brutality," continued Horace. "We were into that early… People weren't used to standing up to the police and talking about respect."

The tensions that had been steadily building reached a critical point in the hot summer of 1965. A Black man named Marquette Frye was taken into custody following a routine traffic offense. The riots that began on August 11 and lasted for six days claimed thirty-four lives as nearly four thousand people were arrested. On May 7, 1966, two cops shot and killed Leonard Deadwyler, an African American man rushing his pregnant wife to hospital. As mirrored in the Rodney King incident almost three decades later, the police were cleared of all charges.

The response from the Black community was to get organized, as music became a tool for change. "The [Arkestra] just happened to be hooked up with the revolutionaries, that's just the way it was," Tapscott told Bob Rosenbaum in an interview. "There was Stokely Carmichael, Rap Brown, the cats, they'd come around and sit around while we'd rehearse and talk about the music." Elaine Brown remembers how culture and politics were inseparable as resistance to the brutality grew: "We were just all there experiencing the same things; in it together with Martin Luther King and Rosa Parks. It was a moment of time where all the forces lined up for the oppressed; so we had no choice but to find each other. There was a tidal wave and you could either get in it and swim, or not, because everyone was caught up in *something* if you were in Los Angeles at that time."

After meeting Horace following her breakdown extenuated by wrongly prescribed drugs, Elaine Brown soon

"This horn is a weapon and I'm prepared to use it like that."
—Lester Robertson

experienced the protective arm of the bandleader. "Horace starting taking me home and making sure I wasn't gonna get killed," she says. "Watts, at that time, was a dangerous place with a whole lot of people with a lot of rage and carrying guns. I was so out of it, I needed to be taken care of, and that became a big part of our relationship."

The authorities were not oblivious to the power of music in the community, as Horace recalled to Michael Slate in an interview in 1996: "You know, the police blamed the Arkestra for the riots. See, in 1965, we was still on 103rd Street at this coffeehouse, a place called Watts Happening… We were out there rehearsing and playing and having classes. We had all kinds of people in these classes. We had people from the Panthers and from all these other kinds of groups… All these people came together when the music was being played." This coffeehouse became the focal point for the Ark and the cultural renaissance that followed the uprising. "All the artists got together, you'd talk about the times, and there was lots of space for performance," bassist Wilber Morris recalled to Isoardi. "All kinds of things: acting, dancing, a big stage for the big band. That was exciting… It was like things are getting better—revolution time."

The increasing attention of the authorities was evidence of the music's revolutionary power. "We got raided by the FBI one day," Horace told Michael Slate. "We were rehearsing and we had thirty-five cats in the band. Upstairs was Rap Brown and some of the cats from back East…. At the rehearsals all the time we'd always see these cars on the corners following different cats."

Elaine Brown thinks Horace was drawn into the political fight as much by circumstance as design. "You've got to remember that the Watts uprisings were a direct response to the inequalities that Blacks suffered in America," she says. "By the time Martin Luther King was killed, there were one hundred cities that exploded. So any kind of Black militancy or Black consciousness or anything that disturbed the status quo was being crushed. So Horace was certainly swept into the whole thing that the FBI was trying to destroy."

While he was most definitely a part of the struggle, Papa, as Tapscott was affectionately known, was not a complete supporter of the Panthers' revolutionary tactics. "Horace was always trying to impose with people not to be violent with each other," says Brown. "He was very patient and always wanted to bring everyone together in a non-antagonist way. Even though we had differences, to have that kind of cool person in this rough area meant he was very respected… He was able to show people that we had a greater interest in being united than being divided and that we had to know who we were. And music was his contribution in helping bring us together around something that would build, and not destroy, community."

Horace Tapscott's connection to the Black Panthers, in the eyes of the authorities, was sealed by a collaboration with Brown, who, as well as being a party activist, was an aspiring singer whom Horace had helped nurture. *Seize the Time,* the 1969 LP the two friends recorded together with members of the Ark, was a powerful cry for liberty and, according to the newspaper the *Black Panther,* contained "the first songs of the American revolution." Elaine Brown recalls how the recording came about. "John Higgins and Bunchy Carter were killed at UCLA, and I was there. It was very traumatic, and I wrote a song about it. Then I sang at the funeral of Bunchy Carter, and the head of the party, David Hilliard, came down and said he wanted to hear my songs. So we went off and got a piano, and he liked one of them in particular ['The Meeting'] and said, 'That's gonna be the Black Panther Party national anthem.' So next thing I knew, he was saying I had to make an album."

The recording sessions for this heavyweight LP were closely monitored. "It was a really rough time," remembers Brown. "The police would come outside the studio, and they would stop people; it was horrible. Because they didn't want this album made. But Horace was totally unmoved by this. Whereas some people would have been full of bravado, he would just focus on the music."

While music became a healing force in the community, others looked back to similarly deep-rooted ancestral traditions. "We had a lot of spoken word," Tapscott told

Isoardi. "People would come in and talk about how they felt about getting beat up by the police that week. They would talk about what happened and how it happened."

The Watts Writers Workshop was the brainchild of screenwriter Budd Schulberg, who wanted to create a forum from where out of "hopelessness might rise a Black phoenix." By the mid-'60s, acclaimed writers like Stanley Crouch and Quincy Troupe were regulars at the workshop, as was Ojenke, one of the first poets to join the UGMA.

Like Tapscott, Anthony Hamilton had experienced the full force of Central Avenue before moving to Watts, where he took on the name Father Amde. Becoming the assistant director of the workshop, he went on to form the mighty Watts Prophets (alongside Richard Dedeaux and Otis O'Solomon), whose contribution to the Black arts is often overlooked in favor of their East Coast counterparts, the Last Poets. Another key L.A. poet to rise out of this scene was Kamau Daáood, who explains how out of the workshop were born two related but distinct schools of spoken word: "The writing of the Watts Prophets was more folk based and came out of the tradition of rhyming couplets and that kind of thing, which is why they became known as the godfathers of hip-hop. And then you had another style, which came out of jazz-based or sermonic traditions and improvisation, which was where Ojenke came in. But one thing that is also important to remember is, you [had] all these cats down in Watts reading Dostoyevsky and Nietzsche, so you had that mixed up with all the militancy. So the movement was not only very oral, performance based, and radical, but also [deep] in terms of imagery and surrealism. It was very deep."

While the Watts Happening Coffee House became a regular focus for the poets to join with the Ark in performance, Kamau Daáood's first experience of working with Horace came at another important venue for the collective. "They used to have regular festivals on Malcolm X's birthday at a place called South Park," he says. "Horace had heard my poetry, so he asked me to come onstage and read before this fourteen-piece orchestra with the horns playing John Coltrane's 'Equinox.' To play in that Ark was like having the angels and the ancestors behind you. It was like being home, and you were in a place where you were supported and loved."

It is both a sign of the Ark's fierce reputation and Horace's unwillingness to compromise that during one of their most serious periods they only recorded one album. The Horace Tapscott Quintet's *The Giant Is Awakened*, released on Flying Dutchman in 1969, was one of the most powerful releases on this label. Talking about the title track, which he wrote in 1964, he told Michael Slate: "'The Giant Is Awakened' was about the people here in this country, and how things was happening to Black folks in this country, and we had to wake up and start to protect and defend and push forward our beliefs and our thoughts and our dreams."

"Then you see them dancing down the street hummin' to 'Dark Tree,' it puts a lump in your throat. I mean, cats eleven to fifteen." —Horace Tapscott

The album also included "The Dark Tree," which had been part of the Ark's set since the early '60s. "Then you see them dancing down the street hummin' to 'Dark Tree,'" Horace recalled to Bob Rosenbaum about how during the insurrections the song had become a rallying cry right across South Central. "It puts a lump in your throat. I mean, cats eleven to fifteen."

Despite critical acclaim, Horace was unhappy with the end result of *Giant* after being kept out of the final mixing process, and it was the nearest he would come to a major-label affiliation. The whole experience increased his mistrust of an industry that would never fully embrace his genius. Unfortunately, unlike other collectives like Strata-East and Tribe, the Arkestra's self-reliance did not expand to a record label. After years of neglect by the industry, however, the Arkestra was eventually taken under the wing of a six-foot, blue-eyed German American named Tom Albach, whose Nimbus label would release the group's finest work. "When he came down into the ghetto, he came down there and said what he had to say, and he got the respect of the cats," Tapscott told Isoardi. "So he's got a niche in the Arkestra that no one White has ever had. He came and told his story, and he took care of a lot of the cats… He helped some cats

(top) In concert at South Park, late 1960s. Photo by Kamau Daáood (bottom left) "Angela Is Happening!" flyer, circa 1970. (bottom right) Leaflet for Arkestra concert, 1976, courtesy of Kamau Daáood.

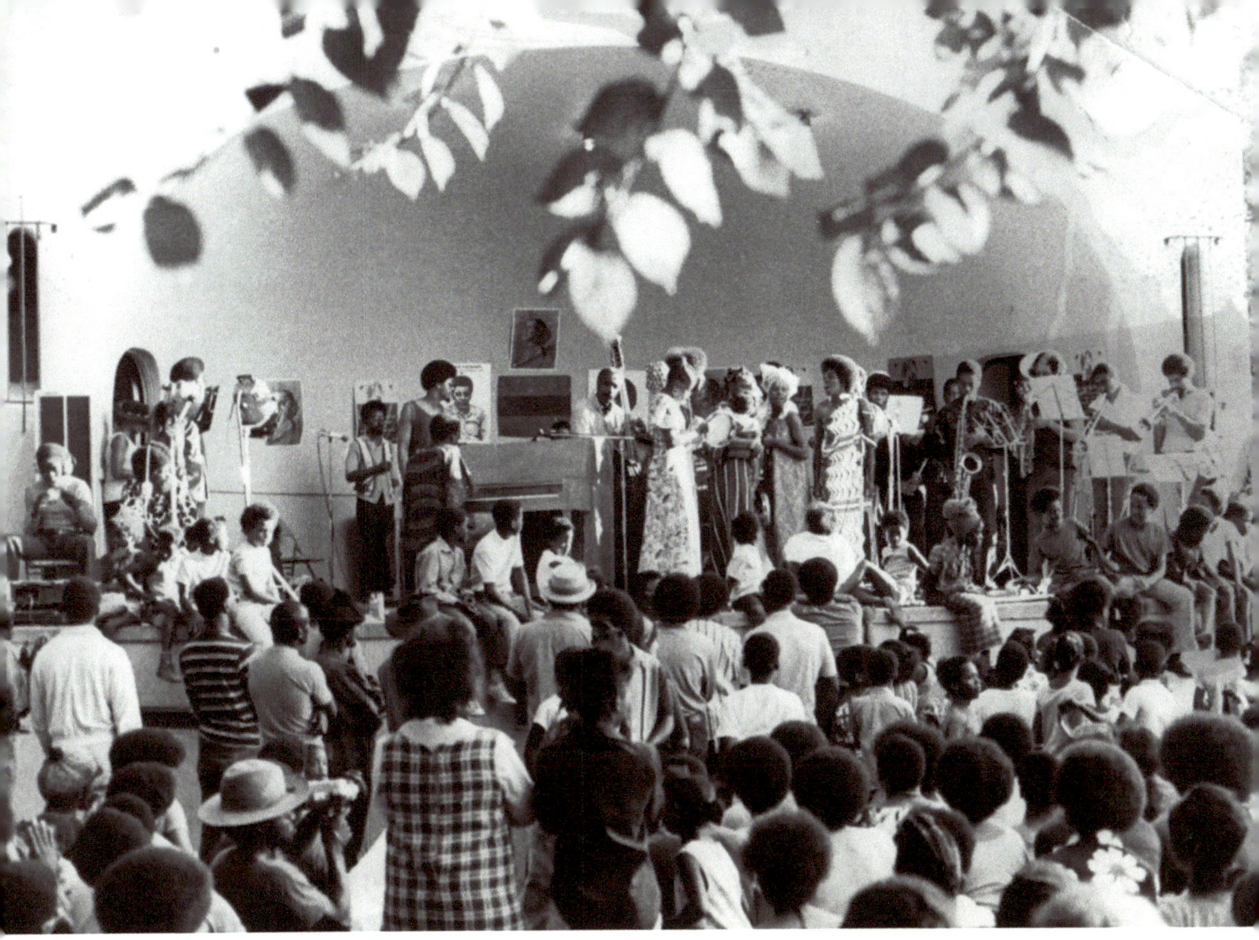

Sponsored by
The Committee of the Arts
to Free Angela Davis
ANGELA IS HAPPENING!
assembled and written by
Elvie Moore
of the Meat Theatre
directed by
Thoma Scott Young
director of
The Meat Theatre
produced by
STREET
the guerilla theatre-street theatre coalition of Los Angeles' most exciting theatre groups
production manager
Mallory Pearce
set design
John Gibson
special contributions:
June Bruno
'Black Culture' poem
Otis Smith
Malcolm X's part
Chuck Nettles
Otis Smith
Martin Luther King's part
Judge
Bob Klonsky
Militant
Roger Mosley
Young Militant
Dave Windom
John Brown
a Friend of the People
Angela
Stephanie Faulkner
Bandaged Woman: Witness at Lynching
Penny Pearce
Frederick Douglass
William Marshall
Harriet Tubman
Shaba Barnes
Tom Paine
Peter Virgo, Jr.
Welfare Woman Frances E. W. Harper
Barbara Jones Bae
All American Racist
Terry Gordon
Wino Poet
Frank Williams
Robert Williams
Craig Duane Stewart
George Jackson
Cal Wilson
Susan B. Anthony
Sandy Buckbinder
W.E.B. DuBois
Michael Shaw
Malcolm X
Richard Dedeaux
Rap Brown
Alan R. Flagg
Che
Mariano Rzasniowieschi
Martin Luther King
Chuck Nettles
Nat Turner
Anthony Sweeting
Crowd Member
Garland D. Minor
Jury
Prominent Citizens
Dee Dee McNeil singing
'Black in a White World,' by Dee Dee McNeil & Marthea Hicks
The Community Cultural Arkestra
'Freedom Suite,' Directed by Horace Tapscott
Mafundi's Community Youth Choir
'Sinner, Where You Going to Run To?' directed by Mrs. Kinney
P.A.S.L.A. Singers
'Free Angela,' composed for this production and directed by Phil Moore
Otis Smith prophet
Black Expression by a Black Man, the Truth Noone Wants'
Exerpts from the film, 'Angela: Portrait of a Revolutionary'
The Watts Prophets
Luther Keyes, poet
'Poem to Myself and Other Niggers (and Anyone Else Who Cares to Listen)
Slides: Researched and Produced by:
Alan Zak
photographer
Third World Motionless Film Council
professional slide show producers: 294-2716, 293-0385
FREE ALL POLITICAL PRISONERS
THINGS TO DO!!!!
Tell the facts to friends - possibly give a fund-raising and-or information party and we'll arrange for speakers and-or performers and literature.
Write to the Attorney General and Governor and demand that this political frame-up be stopped.
arrange to have the play produced - at a school, or as part of a community fund-raising and education effort - as single events or preferably for an extended run.
Show the film 'Angela: Portrait of a Revolutionary' at fund-raising gatherings.
Show the film about the Soledad Brothers.
Join the Committee of the Arts to Free Angela, which sponsored and initiated this happening.
To do all of these things, contact the National United Committee to Free Angela Davis, 3450 West 43d St., Los Angeles 90043, California. (213) 296-4402.
designed and printed by the Peace Press

U.G.M.A.A. FOUNDATION
PAN AFRIKAN PEOPLES ARKESTRA
HORACE TAPSCOTT–CONDUCTOR
GREAT HOUSE CONCERT
2412 S. WESTERN AVE.
LA. CALIF. 90018
SAT. JULY 24,1976
9:00 PM. UNTIL 2:00 PM.
DON. $2.50 PER. PERSON
$4.00 PER. COUPLE
TAX EXEMPT

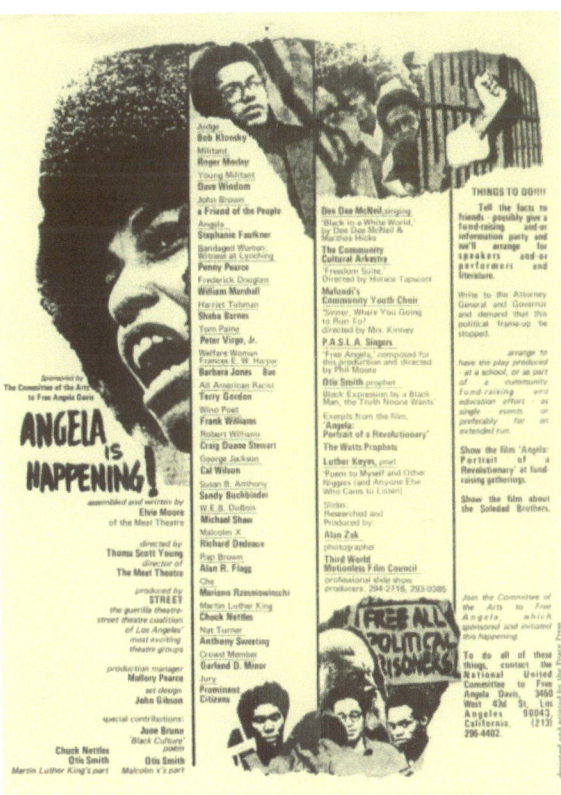

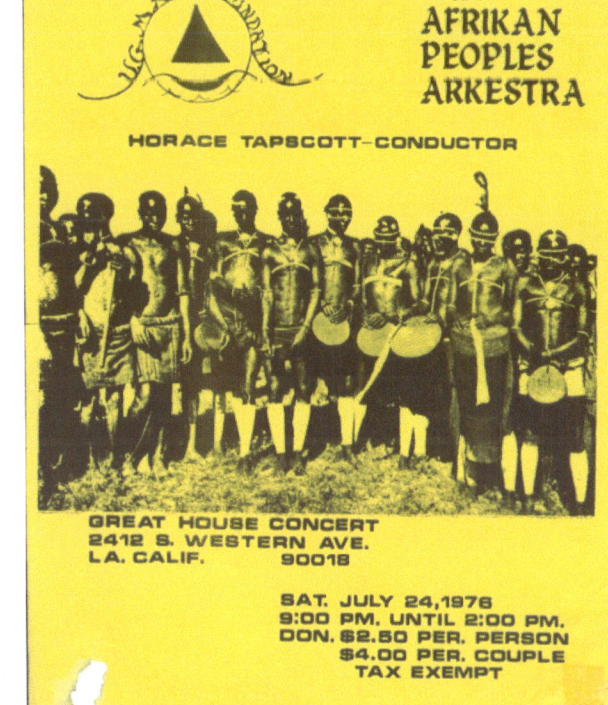

Horace conducting at South Park, late 1960s. Photo by Kamau Daáood.

get back on their feet, that kind of thing. And all those guys never forgot that, you know."

Despite the loss of longtime Ark members such as Arthur Blythe and Butch Morris, the mid-'70s saw the Ark reborn under the leadership of a heavy multi-reed player by the name of Jesse Sharps, who had first encountered the Arkestra at the Coffee House in 1966. Other long-standing members, such as bassist Roberto Miranda and alto saxophonist and future bandleader Michael Session, joined Sharps as the Arkestra reached one of its most creative periods. The late flautist Adele Sebastian explained how one of the Ark's songs, "Quagmire Manor at 5 AM," captured both the mood of their new home and the dedication to their art that Jesse Sharps's discipline had instilled in the group. "I believe that song pretty much tells the story of what the 'Quag' was like around five o'clock in the morning," Sebastian said. "You could find musicians somewhere in the house playing, blowing, letting it all out. And that was beautiful too." Thankfully, Tom Albach was around to capture the creative energy of one of jazz music's great ensembles, releasing the albums *The Call* and *Flight 17* in 1978.

During this period, the Ark was tapping into a cultural force across the nation. "You had all these different movements of artists coming together to form collectives—from St. Louis to Chicago," Kamau Daáood recalls. "So it was about artists of like minds involved in developing their art and, at the same time, having social consciousness and a sense of responsibility."

Throughout the '70s, the Arkestra had played every last Sunday at the Immanuel United Church of Christ on the corner of Eighty-fifth and Holmes. The invite had come from Reverend Edgar Edwards, and the Arkestra was an integral part of the church minister's community outreach program. Recorded between February and June 1979, *Live at I.U.C.C.* (including saxophonist Sabir Mateen's killer spiritual jazz track "Village Dance") is a heavy testament to the freedom and fire of those sessions.

The four Arkestra albums recorded for Nimbus were powerful ensemble works, with the collaborative spirit enhanced through the delegation of writing duties to members of the group. This freedom also led to Ark members branching out to record their own albums on Nimbus. Bassist Roberto Miranda recalls how Horace guided members to reach the peak of their creativity: "Horace was as much a musical mentor as one can be when one leads by love and example. By that I mean, he let you know he loved and respected you, and he played at a very high artistic standard. He led and inspired in the same way. However, if one did not meet the artistic standard he set in his example, he did not discourage them. He smiled that great smile of his and somehow let you know he believed that if you worked hard, you could do it." Tapscott's music had always reached beyond the African American jazz heritage to Latin, Caribbean, and African music, and that was certainly reflected in Nimbus releases of the period such as Miranda's mighty Afro-Latin LP *Raphael*.

Another musician drawn to the collective, Lagos-raised percussionist Najite Agindotan felt the comparisons between Tapscott and another of his own great mentors. "He reminded me exactly of what Fela [Kuti] did," he says in Isoardi's book. Arriving in L.A., Najite found a city with a long heritage of community percussion playing stretching back to late '60s when the drumming circles started in Venice Beach. A veteran of that scene and Ark member Conga Mike recalls what it was like to be creating the rhythmic foundations for the group: "It was a new experience for me, playing with all those horns. I dug it. Horace hardly ever gave me any specific direction except to keep playing. A lot of the tunes lent themselves to traditional conga rhythms; some didn't. It was new for me, playing those tunes with more than one time signature, and those odd time signatures—11/8 and 7/8 and 5/4. I figured out some cadences to play, and kept counting."

While the '80s were a relatively quiet period for the Ark, with a number of members passing on (most notably Adele Sebastian, whose death still hits members hard) and Reaganomics tearing at the social infrastructure, it proved a transitional time for Horace both personally and musically. Following a near-death aneurysm in 1978, he returned to be viewed by many as a different player capable of even deeper music. The solo piano albums he released for Nimbus entitled *The Tapscott Sessions* captured a man at the height of his art and sit there alongside solo releases by piano legends such as Randy Weston and Abdullah Ibrahim. Future Arkestra singer and now member of Build an Ark, Dwight Trible recalls catching one of these solo sessions. "I couldn't believe what I was seeing and hearing," he says. "It was so intense by the time he finished, I was exhausted. I had never seen anybody give that much of themselves."

The ongoing slashing of social support and the flooding of the area with crack cocaine to support the contra army in Nicaragua had left the Black neighborhoods of South Central blighted like never before, as gangs and the LAPD did their best to destroy the area. It would take the televised beating of Rodney King to reveal the truth about what had been happening for years, and to finally tip the community over the edge. "We saw it coming," explained Tapscott to Michael Slate about the 1992 uprisings. "Being here in the community, you saw it from the ground up and you saw where it was going. Eventually it boiled over. And I thought the same as I did in the Watts Rebellion. The reasons why it happened still haven't been addressed correctly."

As South Central burned, a creative haven took root around the Black arts enclave of Leimert Park, as young and old came together to make sense of the madness. "Lester Robertson, my dead partner, used to say, 'First there's shit and then there's the flower. There's concrete and then there is some grass growing out the concrete,'" explained Horace. "We at the point of how do we keep these things, hone these plants up to the point where they blossom into something out of this rock, out of this shit that we in. We in a lot of shit, we in a hard place right now with our youngsters and our oldsters together."

The World Stage, set up by Kamau Daáood and veteran jazz drummer Billy Higgins, and Fifth Street Dick's coffeehouse, the home of Vietnam vet and homeless jazz-and-coffee-obsessive Richard Fulton, sat just a few doors east of Ben Caldwell's KAOS Network, which became the breeding ground for the legendary Project Blowed sessions at the Good Life Cafe. It was only a matter of time before the jazz elders and the hip-hop generation found a common ground. Out of these sessions came the rap group Freestyle Fellowship, whom Horace would go on to both play with and record for. "It was like this," says the group's lyricist Aceyalone. "When the Good Life was going on, it began around eight [and lasted] till ten, but then it starting flowing over until the early hours. And we would take our sessions over to Leimert Park and start jamming with the live bands, so there was a whole load of going back and forth." One of the elders and now grandfather to Aceyalone's daughter, Dwight Trible recalls the energy of the times. "It was so electric every night of the week," he says. "I just loved to go and stand on the corner and breathe the air and see what beautiful surprise would be happening today, and also to stir up the water a bit myself to be a part of a family." Helping make the links between the generations was Jamm Messenger Divine (JMD), who became something of a linchpin for the scene. "The natural connection came through jazz musicians around my way like JMD," Aceyalone recalls. "He was one of the producers who put together the jazz and hip-hop."

Horace described the importance of these creative interactions to Michael Slate: "We bring all the guys together, all the age brackets and all the different kinds of people… And these Black youngsters here have learned how to be together without killing each other or stabbing each other… The system says that's not good. We don't want you strong."

Kamau Daáood was another figure who had experienced the reactions within the arts scene during both insurrections. "One of the things that connects what happened in '65 and '92 is that when people feel they are oppressed, and they rebel," Daáood says. "After they go through those major explosions, they are wide open. Their emotions are wide open, and their minds are wide open, and they need to express themselves. But more importantly, they need to listen to others and to try and make sense of the things around them. So it brought people out to talk to each other and made the community look at itself. And that had happened during both uprisings. So now in '92, you had veterans of the previous time, in the midst of young folks experiencing that kind of situation for the first time in their lives. So with the World Stage and Fifth Street Dick's and all these venues, you had this creative form of the exchange of ideas. It was pretty much the same thing really, the poets and the hip-hop guys, because they were both spokesmen and reporters for what was happening at the time. Soaking up and spitting out what was happening around them."

In a mirror of what happened thirty years before, the focus of the LAPD moved on to the arts. "I wasn't surprised at all by the police invasion that night when they attacked Project Blowed," explained Horace. "It told me and proved to me that the race was getting stronger, coming together stronger. You had all these youngsters on the corner rapping and talking the way they do. Fifty feet away from them was some older guys rapping and one hundred feet from them was some senior cats rapping. All these people out here together, the grandfathers and the grandsons."

Aceyalone speaks for the whole Good Life scene when he talks of the lineage he and his crew became part of. "Leimert Park has been falling into different meanings for different generations," he says. "I think, for our generation, which was the first youthful generation to use Leimert Park and the jazz heritage as an example, we really embrace all that. So our generation knows the World Stage, it knows about Billy Higgins, Kamau Daáood, and of course, it knows about Horace Tapscott."

Back in the '80s, Tapscott recalled what it meant to him to be working across the generations. "I wanted Black people to appreciate their contributions to the culture here. I mean people all over the world knew the contributions Black people made but the Black people here didn't even know; it was kept hidden from them. Today I think these young rap artists got to know the contributions they make. It's to the point today that these young rap artists look to cats like me, in my age bracket, to always remind them that rap is the grandson of the blues. The music started a long time ago. It began when we were first brought here and contributions have been added to the music ever since then."

Visit the corner of Los Angeles where Horace spread his community ethos during nearly forty years, and speak to anyone who met him, and you get an idea of both the power of the man and the loss to the community that his death in February 1999 brought. And looking back on what Horace set out to achieve, one can only feel a sense of the great debt that community owes to their Papa. "I had to get the truth told whether it was accepted or not," Horace once said. "That was my life's thing… It's part of having a stake, making a contribution to this country. We came over here as slaves. We didn't ask to come here but we here now and we made a contribution in spite of all this crud they put us under. We have to be proud of what we did, but we have to know what it was we did. It's very important for me that our people, the young people, can dig themselves and the contributions they can make."

For a man who touched so many in the community, it's fitting that one of those he saved gives the most moving and concise summary of Horace Tapscott's legacy. "First of all, he wrote extraordinary music in the tradition of Mozart and Ellington," concludes Elaine Brown. "While his music has not been heard widely, when people are looking back at the history of jazz, he is in the pantheon of the greats as both a musician and composer, and that has to be recognized. He was a genius, in being able to get all those people together in the orchestra and to inspire all those great people. And then as a man, he was inspirational to a whole lot of people, including me. He was a facilitator who helped people find their way. Anyone who met Horace Tapscott has to say that they could do some stuff that would be good and meaningful to humanity. There was no way you could be around Horace and not be transformed into a better person." .

Andy Thomas is a London-based music writer currently working on his first book, *The Spirit's in It*.

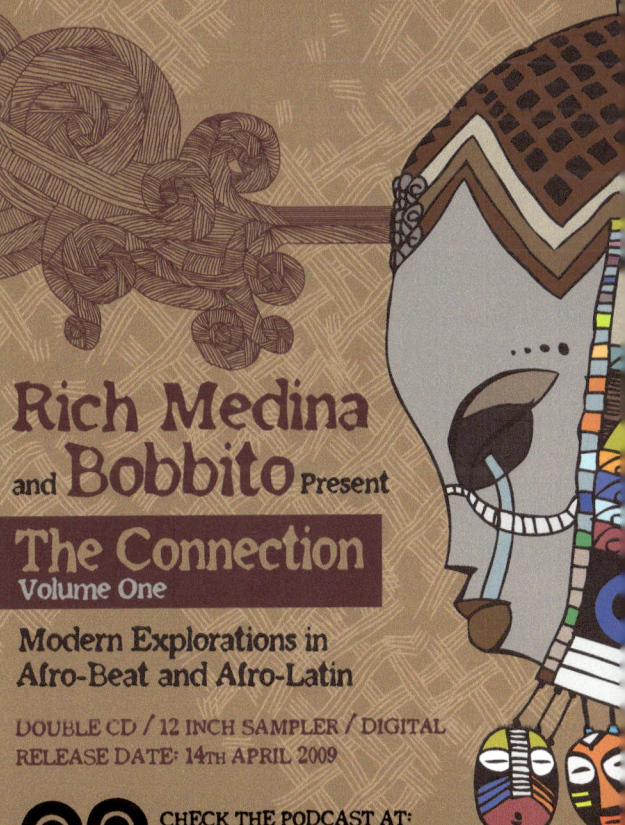

Soul Conductor

Bassist-turned-arranger Richard Evans put the soul in Cadet Records

interview by **David Ma** and **Dan Ubick**,
foreword by **Dan Ubick**

From the late 1960s to the early 1970s, Richard Evans was the main man behind Chicago's groundbreaking soul-jazz record label Cadet, a subsidiary of the successful blues label Chess. In the early '60s, Richard not only took Charles Stepney under his wing but also played bass with Sun Ra and befriended a young, talented organ player named Donny Hathaway. As the '60s neared their end and popular music became more psychedelic, Leonard Chess's son, Marshall, took over the business, and Richard was promoted to full-fledged in-house arranger. He would soon become much more.

Successful LPs by Woody Herman (1970's Grammy-nominated *Light My Fire*), the Soulful Strings, and Marlena Shaw (1969's *The Spice of Life*) brought the fuzz and echo of '60s rock into the mix at Cadet sessions. It also garnered Mr. Evans complete artistic control in terms of signing whomever he wanted (jazz harpist Dorothy Ashby) and producing however he saw fit. He was as fit as Muhammad Ali and most definitely *the man* during Cadet's most fertile period. The results are some of the most sampled and well-respected LPs of the soul era. As Mr. Evans puts it: "I wanted things to be very Black [and] very funky at Cadet."

Richard Evans went on to find even more success at labels like Capitol and Atlantic, producing and arranging LPs for Natalie Cole, Peabo Bryson, Eddie Harris, Ahmad Jamal, Tower of Power, and Ramsey Lewis—but his stint at Cadet is an unmatched legacy. We spoke with the man they now call Professor Richard Evans, who currently instills his years of expertise and insight to young hopefuls at Boston's Berklee College of Music. He's surely still in the mix, and he is still doing it all for his brother, Claude.

Tell us a little bit about your upbringing and when you were first introduced to music.
I was born in Birmingham, Alabama, in 1932, and came to Chicago in 1939. My brother [Claude] came and got me from Birmingham, 'cause he had been in Chicago for a few years already. When we came to Chicago, before World War II, everything was real rural. There were ghettos everywhere. I mention this because I was still able to hear all kinds of music despite being poor. My mother listened to Paul Robeson and Marian Anderson a lot. We'd also listen to the Duke Ellington and Count Basie stuff too. This was before Bird [Charlie Parker], of course. I also remember one of our neighbors had a record player, so I'd listen to blues records too.

We lived in an area in Chicago that had a venue called the Regal Theater. Later, I found out it was part of what they called the chitlin circuit. I remember being about nine years old and going there. You could watch two movies, and then watch Count Basie *live*, Duke Ellington *live*, and Fats Waller *live*. And we loved Fats Waller because at the end of the show, he'd take the curtain, wrap it around his belly, and shake it. [*laughs*] Cab Calloway was there too. I tell you this because, for some reason, we knew we were getting something special and that we were privileged to see these people live.

And if you turned on the radio, you had Al Benson, a Black disc jockey who'd play Black music. And when the Black programming was done, you'd hear Polish programming and their music. And I *never* turned the radio off. I listened to all kinds of stuff. I knew polkas, how they went, and how they sounded. Chicago has the largest Polish population

Illustration by Josh Dunn.

outside of Warsaw, so I absorbed a lot of Polish tunes and their distinct style. My stepfather was [actually] a farmer and began working the steel mill when the war started. When he'd make us breakfast, he'd listen to country music, so that's how I heard country. So I had listened to jazz, the blues, Polish music, and country, *and* Minnie Pearl even.

As a kid, I didn't know I was gonna grow up to be a musician. It just worked out that I came across diverse stuff when I was young. Plus, later I found out I could listen to a song once and arrange it without reading the sheet music.

When exactly did you pick up the bass?
Well, I always knew I was gonna be an artist. My brother was in the service in Guam and wrote me a letter saying I should be a musician. He was a hero to me, and anything he said, I would do. So I took music in high school and decided to play the bass, because it was a quiet instrument. People could *see* me play it but could not really *hear* it, so they wouldn't know that I wasn't a real musician. [*laughs*]

When my brother came out of the Army, he started working the steel mill with my dad. One day, I came home, and in the middle of the living room was a brand-new stand-up bass! My brother had worked two weeks [straight] to save the cash to get me that thing. I said, "Well, I'm gonna let him know he didn't waste his money."

You went on to play with Sun Ra really early on in your career. What was Sun Ra like as a bandleader?
Sun Ra, to my ear, was like a poor man's Duke Ellington at the time. He was like the planet Saturn; he was just strange and far out. He would do magic tricks a lot. And if you were a horn player in his band, he would write licks for you. Also, you couldn't say anything negative to him. It wasn't a band, more like a cult. He was one strict fella.

One time, I painted a sign for him that said "Sun Ra and his fabulous jazz band performing." I spent about two weeks on it. He looked at it and broke out laughing. He said, "We don't play *jazz*, we play *dazz*." I took my little painting back, and still don't know what he meant by that. [*laughs*]

I stayed with Sun Ra for about a month or so. Even though I left his band, and even though he was a strange fella, he did show me how to get copyrights for my work. I have to give him credit for helping me out with that.

CADET RECORDS

In the earlier years, Cadet was called Argo, both subsidiaries of Chess. Your LP, *Richard's Almanac* was for Argo. Describe the main changes from recording for Argo and doing LPs for Cadet.
I think the year was 1959, and I was a whippersnapper then! I had a trio that followed Ahmad Jamal around Chicago, and that's how I became involved with the fellows behind Cadet. I remember the company being located at Twentieth and Michigan Street in a three-story building with a studio in it. Chess did the blues, and Argo did the jazz stuff. The Chess Brothers, Phil and Leonard, were from Poland. They *really* liked Black blues. And at that time, in the '40s, Black music was considered "race music."

The Chess brothers were Polish Jews. And the rumor said that they left Europe to flee Hitler. They would record these Black guys doing the blues and would go down South and sell the records. Black people just didn't seem to have the wherewithal to take their work and turn it into a company and control their own art—but the Chess brothers did. You see, when World War II broke out, there was a great migration up the Mississippi River to Chicago and Detroit to work in the war plants. So a lot of Black folks brought along with them their music. The Chess brothers saw and knew that.

What were the feelings towards the Chess brothers' selling Black music? Was it seen as a negative or positive thing?
Anyone who *was* White and took the time to appreciate our music, like the Chess brothers genuinely did, we appreciated it. The attitude towards someone doing things with Black music was: "I'm glad *someone's* doing it."

You worked at Cadet during its heyday from 1967 to '70. Was it a conscious idea to incorporate more current production techniques and sounds (fuzz, tape delay, et cetera) into the Cadet model?
Yes, mostly. But I never got into that whole psychedelic scene, because I made up my mind as a young person that I wanted to live to be a hundred. So I never did drugs or anything. I mean, cocaine makes your heart beat faster, and I believe your heart only has so many beats it can beat. [*laughs*]

My point is, when the Rolling Stones got popular, Marshall, son of Leonard Chess, started hanging around with 'em and got into doing drugs. When his father Leonard passed away in fall of 1969, Marshall took over and wanted to make Chess a rock company. That's how a lot of that psychedelic stuff happened on those recordings.

What level of control over what made it to tape did you have? How much of an influence did the Chess

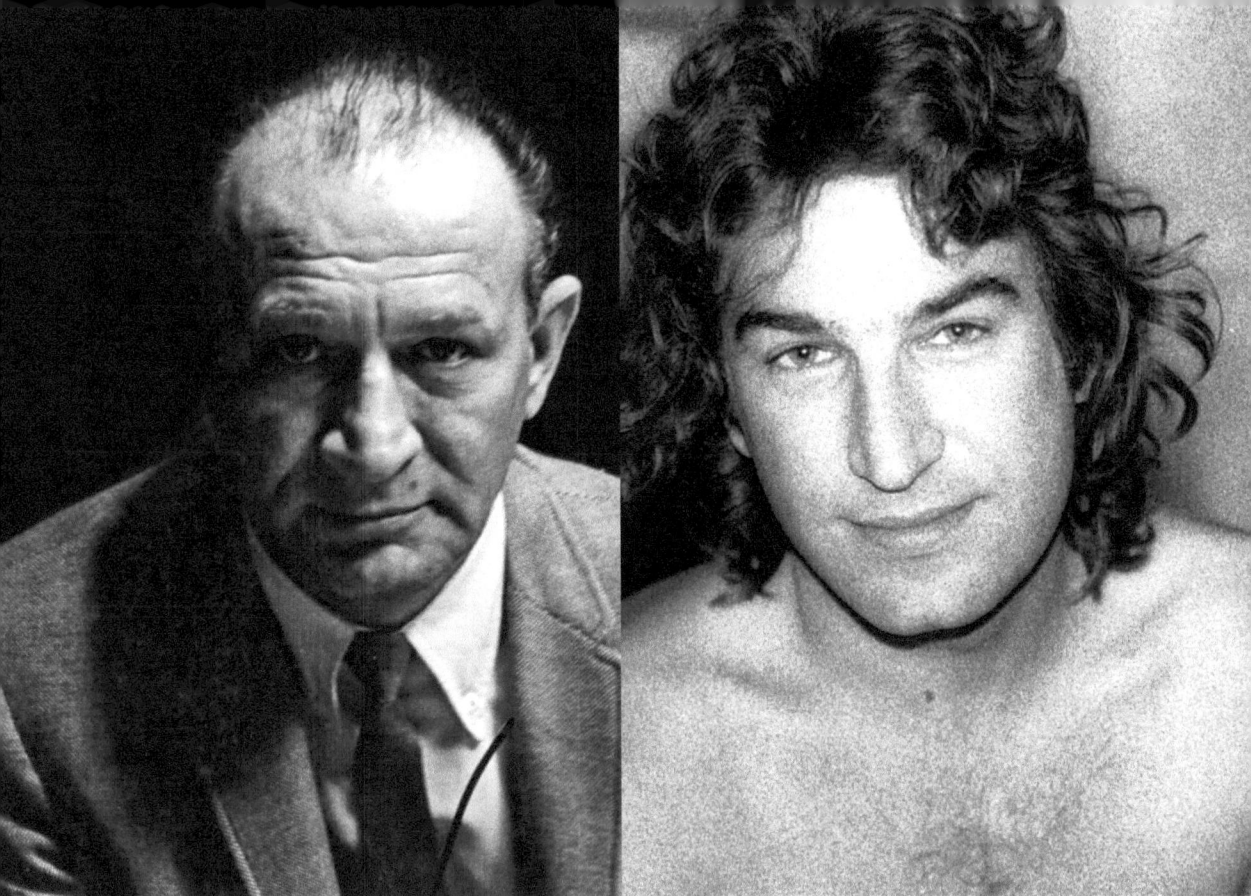

(left) Leonard Chess. (right) His son Marshall Chess. Photograph: Michael Ochs Archive/Getty Images.

brothers have in Cadet?

I had a total free hand to do whatever I wanted there. It was all on me, and they made it clear—sign whomever, fire whomever, and write in whatever style.

Dick LaPalm was an Italian brother who hooked me up [with] Woody Herman. In '67, Woody wanted to work for Chess, and I signed him because Dick wanted me to. On that very same evening, Leonard Chess called me and said, "You signed that old fade Woody?" I told Leonard that I could still get a hit out of him. So we went to a hotel ballroom in North Chicago and rehearsed some songs. We only had four tracks: one track for reeds, one for rhythm, one for solos, and one for brass. We cut that whole album, *Light My Fire,* in two and a half hours. It turned out to become a Grammy-nominated album. Leonard Chess actually passed in '69, so he didn't get to see it being nominated.

So the only guy who had any influence at this time was Dick LaPalm. He actually came out with the idea for [Woody Herman's] *Heavy Exposure*. I credit Dick and myself for bringing Woody's career up at the time. Woody was really overjoyed.

What made the Ter-Mar studio so successful?

All the stuff that was done at Chess Records was done in that studio. Check it out: On a Monday, they'd have Ramsey Lewis cover "The Weight" by the Band. By Wednesday, [we] would press it and be basically done by Thursday. They had a pressing plant on Twenty-first Street to make albums and singles. Chess had the ability to think of a single on Monday, record it the next day, get it made, and have it in stores by Friday.

DONNY HATHAWAY

What are your fondest memories of Donny Hathaway as a man and a musician?

I was with Donny in a car in 1965 or so, before he was *real* famous. We were on our way to a gig. He'd talk about how unpopular he was in school and how people made fun of him. I mean, he was from the South and always kinda had a football-shaped head with a little saddle in the middle of it. [*laughs*] He wasn't ugly or anything, but just had a funny-shaped head. Donny *was* a sensitive guy though. But his wife was a beautiful woman, who could play classical piano and sing. His daughters were beautiful girls too. He was a special guy who had a special way

of *hearing* and *playing* music. Donny could write from a classical standpoint as well.

That's why, when I did Woody Herman's record, *Heavy Exposure*, I brought Donny onto it. Woody didn't know who Donny was, but I told him to just wait. I also brought him onto [Soulful Strings'] *String Fever* too.

So was that Donny humming along with the melody on "Valdez in the Country"?
If anyone's humming on that track, it's Donny.

You, Ric Powell, and Phil Upchurch wrote "Voices Inside (Everything Is Everything)," which ended up on Donny's *Live* LP. Talk a little bit about that song.
What happened was, after he became famous and said he wanted to rerecord "Voices Inside" but that he wanted to change the name to "Everything Is Everything," I said okay. The rest is history. I still get checks for that now.

I supported Donny heavily. In fact, later on he wanted me to be his main producer on another album of his, but I was signed to Chess and couldn't do it. Around that time was actually when his health deteriorated heavily.

When was the last time you saw Donny Hathaway?
In January '79 or so, I saw Donny at the airport with a man on either side of him helping him walk, and he saw me and just sheepishly nodded. About a week later, Rodney Robertson and I were eating dinner and was told that Donny either was pushed out, or jumped out, from a window and had just died. I knew that his mind was going on full speed all the time.

What was going on with him?
Say you're a cop and you go out on an emergency call because someone says they saw a man with a gun. You get there and see a shadow of someone with a gun, and you jump and fire at the shadow! But later, [you] come to find out it was a ten-year-old kid with a toy gun. Those are the kind of experiences that change you; you'll never be the same after that. So Donny, I think, had some bad experiences like that, which messed with his reality.

He was a beautiful human being. I think that he was an all-around genius. If he had lived, the whole music world would have been changed.

TERRY CALLIER

What's your history with Terry Callier?
In 1978, I was supposed to do an album with Terry called *Fire on Ice*. But all of a sudden, in the middle of it, he became very paranoid. It came time for him to put some top vocals onto some of the recordings, and he told me he didn't trust me. Then I get a call from one of his cohorts telling me he's in L.A. and that the session is over. He was wild.

Then, after I told him I was gonna scrap the whole thing, he appears out of nowhere. [*laughs*] So he came back, and we got Minnie Riperton to do some vocals on the project—which was the last time I ever did anything with her. And that was it. I didn't talk to Terry for decades after.

In '95, I got a call from Terry from London, saying he wanted me to produce his new project. I told him I'm not gonna work on his album until I got an official notice from the company. I guess he had some sort of epiphany between those twenty years or so. [*laughs*]

MARLENA SHAW AND CHARLES STEPNEY

"Woman of the Ghetto" is one of your most well-known songs. Give us a little insight about the song.
It was 1968. I lived in an upscale middle-class part of Chicago. By then, I pretty much ran Chess and Cadet. At that time, there was a lot of Black discontent. There was a guy named Bobby Miller who helped write the song, but I didn't like him because he was very arrogant. Anyways, Marlena's albums always did *good*, but not *great*.

Then in 1999, about thirty years later, I got a check in my mailbox. Now look, I believe in a supreme being, not necessarily in churches. If the supreme being can hear you in church, then you can pray from your home. And there were points between the '60s and '90s that I prayed for some relief. So the check was for $75,000, and on it was written "Remember Me." I didn't know what it was about, but I put it in the bank and thought, "I'll argue about it later."

A week later, I get a call from Marlena Shaw asking me if I got a check. She explained that it was for "Woman of the Ghetto," which was on a compilation or remix project in Europe called *Remember Me*. I couldn't believe it.

The hip-hop generation knows you from Marlena Shaw's take of "California Soul" (written by Ashford and Simpson, sampled by Gang Starr and DJ Shadow). What do you remember about making that now-beloved song?
I cannot tell you. I know I produced that album, and I think Charles Stepney produced some of the stuff too. I don't even remember doing the song. I met Charles Stepney in 1962. I

met him through Eddie Harris, who had been ranting and raving about him for a while. Stepney and I ended up doing "Dance of the Sugar Plum Fairy" around '62 or '63. But around '65, he wanted to quit doing music. I told him he had talent and should keep arranging, so he gave it one more shot and ended up doing Minnie Riperton's record. He got in tight with Marshall Chess, and he became the man afterwards.

For my third Soulful Strings project, *Another Exposure*, Charles covered Aretha Franklin's ["Since You've Been Gone"] track on that. Instead of using that as the single, I chose "The Stepper," and that pissed Charles off. After that, our relationship was a bit strained.

In 1976, he passed away. But before that, I got on his case and said, "Man, you're working too hard; you gotta get someone to copy your stuff." I guess he was worried about them stealing his work. I think he just overworked himself.

SOULFUL STRINGS

Tell us how the Soulful Strings projects began.
I went with [saxophonist/composer] Paul Winter in 1962 for a six-month trip for President Kennedy's culture exchange tour. So I was told if I went and played bass, I could do some production and some of my songs will be released once I got back. We ended up being the first jazz band to play at the White House.

Paul hooked me up with Ahmad Jamal, who I had known from a long time before. Ahmad said, "Oh, you're an arranger now? Arrange my next album," and I jumped at the chance, of course. I do recall that when we were doing Jamal's record, they told me I could use what I wanted to, so I got a symphony orchestra. I was writing stuff for instruments I had never even heard of before. [*laughs*]

When Esmond Edwards came in to produce at the time, it was his first production gig. We were into about the fourth cut, and Ahmad just stopped to read some notes he had or something. Edwards got on the mic and said, "Ahmad, cut out the bullshit, and let's get back to work!" I knew that Ahmad Jamal is one of the most sensitive people in this world. Sure enough, Ahmad stopped the session and just walked out on a house full of musicians I'd just hired. He made Esmond leave and refused to work until Esmond was out of the project. So Ahmad and I had to do the mixing and everything ourselves. We had to learn [that] on the spot, and so I never really liked how that album turned out.

But because of that record, I went onto Chess and did all that. I spoke with Leonard Chess and told him I wanted to be an in-house arranger. That was in fall of '62. Leonard said, "Wait till January." I called him back, and Esmond was on the phone. Esmond made me explain to him why I called, and he told me that they didn't need an in-house arranger. "Up yours!" he told me. We exchanged words, and I got a call from Leonard months later telling me about an idea to have strings do up-tempo, contemporary-sounding tunes. So that whole Soulful Strings recordings happened by accident.

Tell us about that funky rhythm section on the Soulful String LPs.
I can only remember Lenny Druss on flute and that he could play anything that had a mouthpiece on it. Lenny was a real sweetheart of a guy. So his girlfriend and his daughter would come to my house and we'd barbecue, and his girlfriend told me that Lenny had told her [that] the best thing that happened to him was playing music with me. And I told her I felt the same doggone way.

Also, Phil Upchurch was on guitar. Ron Steele was a young White kid I had on guitar too, but he did most of the reading for us. See, Phil couldn't read or write music, so everything he did was by ear. You would just give him the chord changes and let him do things just by using his instinct. So I knew my flute and my guitar would be a driving force behind these records.

I also had Johnny Griffith on piano at times. You couldn't work with him too long, because he'd play so fast, he'd wear you out. He said he didn't like all the free jazz because he felt they didn't respect chord changes enough.

So I had Lenny, Druss, Phil, and Johnny. I also worked with [vibraphonist] Bobby Christian by the time we did Soulful Strings' *The Magic of Christmas* album. No one got jealous about solos and stuff, and everyone knew what they needed to do—that's why everything with those sessions worked so well. I used everyone according to their talent.

Where did you find strings players who could swing like that?
The strings weren't necessarily the funky parts of the music. The guitar or flute would be the ones that would groove a lot more. I would just mask the songs with swinging instruments, but it wasn't necessarily the strings that would be funky.

What would you say was your biggest hit for the

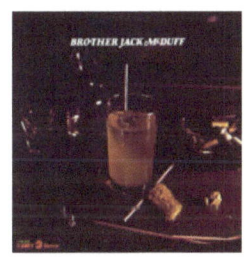

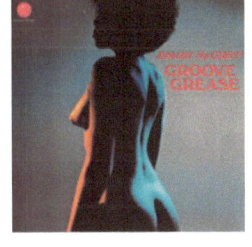

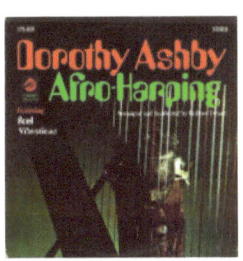

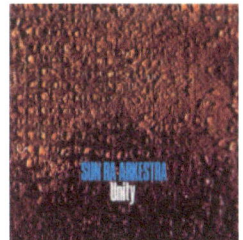

Soulful Strings albums?
My biggest hit was [1967's] "Burning Spear," I would say. It was done [a few years] after Kenya became a sovereign country, so I came up with that track. When that song was released, people started using the song for their radio shows, and it sort of became an anthem. By then, I was running Cadet fully. And after they assassinated Martin Luther King, and with all the race tension going on, people told me I was gonna get in trouble for using so many White musicians on that record. But to me, you could be a zebra for all I care. As long as you could play and understand what I wrote, it didn't matter. Just play my song, and I'll love you.

Why didn't you play bass on those sessions?
Well, I was a mostly a producer at the time, so I didn't want to worry about playing in on a song and be wondering what everyone else sounded like.

If you have [*Soulful Strings Play Gamble-Huff*], there's a track called "I've Got the Groove," which I played bass on. It was a bass with guitar strings on it. It was almost like a cello, so I tuned it in fourths, not fifths. That's me, running the track at half speed, and playing a solo on it. So when you run the track back at regular speed, it sounds real unique and even kind of strange. Other than that, I mainly produced and arranged those records.

Talk about your experience recording the *Back by Demand* LP.
It was in 1968, at the London House [in Chicago]. We played there twice and packed the place. We were guys wearing tuxedos and playing funk. People loved it!

Earlier, you touched on your Christmas album, *The Magic of Christmas*. The version of "Jingle Bells" has by far the funkiest drums on any holiday record. Was it Morris Jennings on the drums?
Lenny told me that his daughter finally heard "Jingle Bells," and she said they weren't playing the melody right. [*laughs*] And it *was* Morris on drums.

DOROTHY ASHBY

Where did you first hear Dorothy Ashby, and when did you know you wanted to work with her?
It was 1962, and I was in New York negotiating with John Hammond, and we were about to watch Ella Fitzgerald. I decided to run to this bar next door, and when I came back, there was this beautiful Black lady with a bass and harp, and I thought I had died and gone to heaven. She really amazed me. I went up to her and told her I really enjoyed her stuff.

In 1966 or so, I went to Detroit to watch [singer/guitarist] Frank D'Rone. When I went to dinner, I saw Dorothy again playing with another trio at the restaurant I was meeting Frank at. Right then, I asked her if she had a record deal. She said no, and I asked her if she wanted one, and that was it. Then we did *Afro-Harping* right after.

From Dorothy's first LPs to *Afro-Harping* and *The Rubaiyat of Dorothy Ashby* on Cadet, the sound changed from straightahead jazz to a very vibey, almost cinematic soul with jazz flourishes. What inspired you to take Dorothy's recording aesthetic to these new realms?
Her jazz playing was very New York-ish, very sophisticated. But I wanted things to be very Black, very funky at Cadet. She had a lot of pentatonic scales and stuff, but I wanted a *swing*. She was an expert on the harp and did things very instinctively. I think she just wanted to please me, and that's why those recordings are different. By the time we cut her last record, it was very artistic. I thought it was gonna sell five copies. [*laughs*] But after those three albums with her, I had to use her anytime I needed a harp player.

Did you keep in touch with Dorothy in her later years?
No, we didn't really keep in touch. But I do remember her as a very modest person. She always had a very self-acquired peace about her. Her manner was very gentle.

After having a wonderful career, working with fascinating musicians, you now teach at Berklee College of Music. Is there a secret to your longevity and vitality?
My secret is that most of the music I did, everything I played and created, was to please my brother, Claude Evans. All of it has been for Claude. ⭕

Dan Ubick is producer/musician, record collector, amateur surfer, and father of two. Wax Poetics previously featured his pieces on Lalo Schifrin and the Gabor Szabo Quintet's Jim Stewart.

David Ma is a regular contributor to Wax Poetics, and has written for various publications including *Remix*, Pitchfork, *The Metro*, *Scratch*, *SLAP*, and *XLR8R*.

Fitz Gore & The Talismen

Jamaican born saxophonist Fitz Gore shines light on this new compilation.

Exotic 70's spiritual Jazz lifted from three rare private pressed albums from Germany.

Limited release out now on CD & LP!

Please check jazzaggression.com/fitzgore for how to order, distribution, sound clips, background story, pictures and more!

PLASTIC STRIP

1ST RELEASE ON ACADEMY LPS REISSUE LABEL: 1973 PSYCHEDELIC AFRO-ROCK CLASSIC

Academy LPs CDs

Ofege — TRY AND LOVE

FROM THE ACADEMY RECORD STORES OF NYC

Listen at: www.myspace.com/academylps

COMING SOON:

THE MEBUSAS "BLOOD BROTHERS"

S.J.O.B. MOVEMENT "A MOVE IN THE RIGHT DIRECTION"

ALL TITLES FULL LICSENED
CONTACT: ACADEMYLPS@GMAIL.COM

OUT NOW

PROJECT: MOONCIRCLE PRESENT: SILENT IN TRUTH COMPILATION 2009 2xLP CD DIGITAL

- DOOM DDAY ONE
- JOHN ROBINSON
- THEMATIK JAHBITAT
- J WINKS CARLO
- T YOUNG MR COOPER
- TEN LOCKE AND MORE

ga digital / groove attack

projectmooncircle.com myspace.com/projectmooncircle

Tune in and listen to a man and his mission!
aka Lil' Sci from Scienz of Life is back...

John Robinson featuring **Lewis Parker**
Limited 7"
a place called home

Join Robinson and Parker as they collectively paint a picture of their foundation habitat backed by a Mr. Cooper sound scape. Lyrics to go!

Release Date: 3rd of April

PROJECT: MOONCIRCLE · HHV Music and Clothing · CROSSTALK

OUT NOW ON LP
THE GRAMMY AWARD WINNING ALBUM
DR JOHN & THE LOWER 911
CITY THAT CARE FORGOT

Featuring guest artists
ERIC CLAPTON · WILLIE NELSON
ANI DIFRANCO · TERENCE BLANCHARD
and includes the hit **TIME FOR A CHANGE**

deluxe heavyweight double vinyl LP
available from
www.diverserecords.com

DIRTY DRUMMER

DIRTY'S MOBILE BEAT SHACK

Dirty's Mobile Beat Shack
15 HipHop, AfroBeat, Dub, Downtempo, Funk Nuggets
Available Everywhere on 4/20

ropeadope
✱ WWW.ROPEADOPE.COM ✱
dirtydrummer.com ✱ myspace.com/thedirtydrummer

Get a Free Dub Sack*
(New Dub inspired beat disc "Dirty's Mobile Dub Sack")
with digital download from ropeadope.com
*limited release, while supplies last

Since 1939

Manufacturing Since 1939...

We still press vinyl records and replicate **DVD** & **CD** discs—in-house.

7", 10", 12" Vinyl Pressing

180 Gram Vinyl • Picture Discs • Colored Vinyl • Custom Packaging

> **New Customers: Get a 5% Discount on your First Order!**
> Mention code "RainWax" to the receptionist when you call in.
> Discount based on Rainbo's standard price sheet. Offer good til September 30th, 2009.

RAINBO RECORDS

8960 Eton Ave., Canoga Park, CA 91304
(818) 280-1100 • Fax: (818) 280-1101
www.rainborecords.com info@rainborecords.com

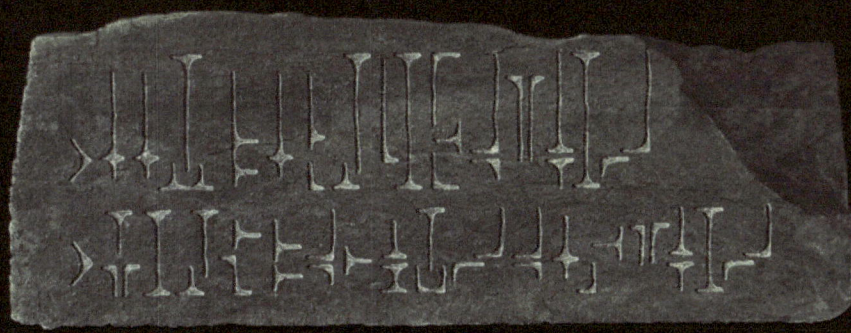

DOOM "BORN LIKE THIS"

MARCH 24th 2009

A NEW ALBUM FROM THE HIP HOP SUPERVILLAIN PREVIOUSLY KNOWN AS MF DOOM FEATURING GHOSTFACE, RAEKWON, PRINCE PAUL, KURIOUS BEATS BY J DILLA, MADLIB, JAKE ONE and DOOM

www.lexrecords.com myspace.com/mfdoom

VADIM MUSIC FRANCE PRESENTS ★★★★★★★★★★
RARE GROOVES & REISSUES
★★★★★★★★★★★ **MARCH 2009**

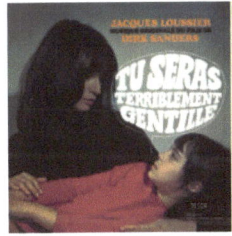  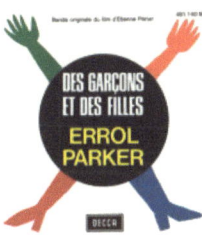 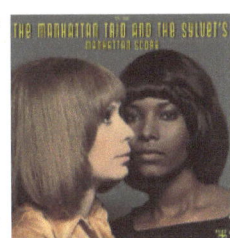 

JACQUES LOUSSIER
OST "Tu seras terriblement gentille" (1968) LP

ROLAND VINCENT
OST "Delphine" (1968) EP

ERROL PARKER
OST "Des garçons et des filles" (1967) EP

THE MANHATTAN TRIO & THE SYLVET'S
"Manhattan score" (1970) SP

MICHEL LEGRAND
"Archi-Cordes" (1964) LP

From original master tapes (LP&7")
Heavyweight Vinyl 180-gram (LP)
Limited edition. Numbered (LP&7")
Original artworks.

  O.S.T. Aéropostale

Worldwide mailorder service for authentic groove. Delivered right to your door
Record shops, contact us for more details.
vadimmusic.com / store@vadimmusic.com / myspace.com/chezvadimmusic

RECORD AUTEUR

Producer Creed Taylor cast strong jazz talent for his personal masterpieces

text **Devin Leonard**

"Simply put, jazz critics are not my favorite people," says Creed Taylor. "And I'm not their favorite producer."

The legendary founder of CTI Records, the great '70s jazz record label, sits in the H2O Grill, a restaurant near his apartment by the East River in Manhattan. Taylor turns eighty this year. You'd never know this is the same man whom his former artists describe as both a creative genius and dictator in the recording studio. He is cordial and unfailingly polite. The seminal jazz record producer seems more like someone you'd meet in the accounting department of a big label.

Still, you get a feeling for Taylor's passion when he defends his work at CTI. He knows the jazz purists preferred label heads like Prestige's Bob Weinstock or Blue Note's founders Francis Wolff and Alfred Lion, who were hands off. They were perfectly happy to document Art Blakey and Miles Davis in the studio with their road bands playing material honed on their nightly gigs. That wasn't Creed Taylor's approach. He was an auteur who used CTI artists like trumpeter Freddie Hubbard, guitarist George Benson, and saxophonists Stanley Turrentine and Grover Washington Jr. to achieve *his* musical vision. "Creed was a real producer," laughs flutist Hubert Laws, another CTI mainstay. "Some of these guys—I'm not going to say their names—come along asking for producer credit after you've got the project finished."

This is what really rankled critics: CTI albums reflected Taylor's personality as much as those of his musicians. The producer had favored high concepts. He produced George Benson's *White Rabbit*, which is really a flamenco jazz record.

Creed Taylor, 1964. Photo by Chuck Stewart.

He mixed jazz with classical music on flutist Hubert Law's *Rite of Spring*, and Deodato's *Prelude* with its hit version of Richard Strauss's "Also Sprach Zarathustra," better known as the theme from the movie *2001*. Taylor recorded Freddie Hubbard playing Paul McCartney's psychedelic "Uncle Albert/Admiral Halsey" and jazz-age cornetist Bix Beiderbecke's impressionistic "In a Mist."

The critics were right about one thing: Taylor sometimes obscured the work of CTI's artists with his eccentricities. He tarted their albums up with glossy string and brass overdubs that smacked of Hollywood. But more often than not, the records were marvelous. He had a gift for putting the right players together in the studio. His soloists were some of the finest in the jazz world. His rhythm sections were the absolute best. The grooves on Taylor's records were impeccable. "I think what Creed learned along the way was to trust the rhythm section," says Ron Carter, the CTI house bassist. "He trusted us to make those arrangements work."

The result was a new genre of sophisticated jazz funk. "He was a genius," says Bob James, a CTI house arranger and pianist who launched his hugely successful career as a solo artist with Taylor. In less than half a decade, Creed made dozens of dazzling jazz albums that transformed the careers of his artists. "He made George Benson a star," said Freddie Hubbard. "He made me a star."

If only it could have lasted longer. In 1974, *Billboard* magazine named CTI jazz label of the year. Then it all came crashing down in an orgy of lawsuits and recriminations. This is the story of the spectacular rise and fall of Creed Taylor and CTI Records.

Creed Taylor: I grew up in Bedford, Virginia, literally two mountain ranges from Bristol, Tennessee, where the Carter Family lived. They invented bluegrass. Anyway, at this high school close to where I grew up, I saw Bill Monroe, the Carter Family, all those guys. I didn't really like that kind of music.

I also heard the big bands that came through. Benny Goodman, Woody Herman, Louis Jordan. That's where I discovered jazz. Then I discovered Birdland. I could pick up Symphony Sid's show on the radio after midnight. I heard him describing all the activities at Birdland. He'd say, "There's Dizzy talking to Kai Winding. I wonder what they are talking about? And meanwhile, Miles's group is on the bandstand." I had my own private earshot into what was going on in New York.

Why did it appeal to me so much? Why do some people like pork chops smothered in onions? I wish I could verbalize it. I just loved the music. Then I heard these 12-inch Jazz at the Philharmonic records in the early '50s while I was at Duke University. They were not very well recorded, and they had interminable solos. At the same time, I bought a 10-inch Zoot Sims record on Prestige or Blue Note. I thought, "That sounds really good." I thought that I'd like to make records that were as exciting as Jazz at the Philharmonic records and sounded as good as the ones on Prestige or Blue Note.

I wanted to be a trumpet player. But I decided shortly after I hit New York that I didn't want to spend my life as a studio musician. But I knew what I wanted to do in the recording studio—even though I'd never been in the recording studio.

A friend of mine had talked this young Swiss guy into founding Bethlehem Records. They were recording big-band stuff and getting deeper and deeper into the hole. I went by the office in New York in 1954 and said, "I can make some records that will sell." I started hanging out at Charlie's Tavern, where I met folks like Quincy Jones, who became a good friend. He helped me put together small groups. Then I'd take them out to Rudy Van Gelder's studio the next day in New Jersey to record them. Word got around. Musicians started saying, "We should listen to this guy, because the records are working out."

In 1956, I went to ABC-Paramount, where I made all kind of records. I recorded flamenco stuff. I did college drinking songs. I even did Chinese music. It's an experience, doing a record. You think how it's going to sound, and you're wondering if people out there are going to like it.

These records sold so well that ABC-Paramount let Taylor start a new jazz label at the company called Impulse. One of the first artists he signed was saxophonist John Coltrane.

Creed Taylor: "It was a case of being in the right place at the right time. Coltrane was coming out of his contract at Atlantic. I'd known him from many long nights at the Village Vanguard. The whole record company would want to sign him. He could have gone with anybody. But we got together. He'd known my productions for a long time. He was very quiet. Once

Bill Evans. Photo by Roberto Polillo.

he kicked his habit, he became very religious, very devout. The two things in his life were religion and music. Musicians told me that when they went out to his house on Long Island, if he was practicing, they'd have to sit out in the living room and wait until he finished. If they had to wait half an hour, so be it. It was like entering the temple of Coltrane. I guess there's how he mastered his sheets of sound. I produced his first record for Impulse, *Africa/Brass*. I thought we should do something different, not the usual tenor sax, trumpet, trombone, rhythm-section date. Any minute detail that I suggested, Coltrane agreed with. I wasn't trying to change the way he spoke through the saxophone. Eric Dolphy was the arranger. He was very open-minded. If I had something valid to suggest, he was more than happy to do it. That helped the session a great deal. Coltrane just played. He left the arranging to Eric and the production to me. He was a very nice person if you can just walk away from the God-like image that's been created for him.

Shortly thereafter, Verve hired Taylor away from ABC-Paramount in 1961.

Creed Taylor: I could hardly wait to start recording all the talented players they had—Stan Getz, Johnny Hodges, and Jimmy Smith. I signed Bill Evans. We did *Conversations with Myself* [the Grammy Award–winning record where the pianist overdubbed three keyboard parts]. You know, if anybody talks when that record is on, it just infuriates me. You have to listen to that record. It takes concentration. Bill was an intellectual with very definite political opinions—Democrat, left of center—which I go along with to this day. And we had the same musical tastes. The only thing about Bill was his habit. He'd come by my office and pick up promos from my secretary. One night, I went up to 125th Street to talk to a disc jockey at a bar. Along came Bill with a box of promos. He was peddling them to the guys at the bar. That saddened me. But I got over it.

And Stan Getz? I'll never forget back when I was in college walking across the campus with my transistor radio and hearing that Stan Getz solo on Woody Herman's "Early Autumn." That sound, that marvelous pleading sound! It just appealed to me. And his vibrato was, like, wow!

I only had one bumpy occasion with him. It was at

Webster Hall when we were recording *Focus* [Getz's famous 1961 Verve record with strings arranged by Eddie Sauter]. Stan showed up at 10:00 AM with a quart of Dewar's and a bottle of Alka-Seltzer. He went into the studio and put the Dewar's on the floor and the Alka-Seltzer up on a stool. After about an hour into the date, he started getting very disagreeable. I just said, "I don't want to record today." We came back another day. Stan was fine. It was a beautiful album—just Stan with a string orchestra. We had [drummer] Roy Haynes on one cut, but he was just playing a snare with brushes.

But Stan was a strange fellow. He won a Grammy in 1963 for best jazz soloist for "Desafinado" on Stan Getz/Charlie Byrd *Jazz Samba* [the Verve album produced by Taylor that introduced bossa nova to the American public]. He didn't want to come with me to the Grammys to get it. He said, "You take it." He wasn't even that thrilled with the tune. It didn't matter. He could play "Old McDonald Had a Farm" and make it sound fantastic.

Soon after, Taylor produced the saxophonist's *Getz/Gilberto*, which spawned the hit single "The Girl from Ipanema." The album went on to win Grammys for best album and best single in 1964. Taylor was named producer of the year at the awards ceremony in New York City. There, he met Herb Alpert and Jerry Moss, founders of A&M. They ended up hiring him to create his own house jazz label at their company. The name: CTI—Creed Taylor Incorporated.

This is where the famous CTI style emerged. Taylor personally oversaw every aspect of the production process. He signed artists like trombonists J. J. Johnson and Quincy Jones, Brazilian composer Antonio Carlos Jobim, guitarist Wes Montgomery, and saxophonist Paul Desmond. He recorded them at Rudy Van Gelder's studio. More often than not, he hired pianist Herbie Hancock, bassist Ron Carter, drummer Grady Tate, and Brazilian percussion wizard Airto to back them up in the rhythm section. He enlisted Don Sebesky to sweeten the results with strings and brass. (Sebesky would later do the same on famous CTI albums by Hubert Laws, Freddie Hubbard, and George Benson.)

Creed Taylor: Here's the way Don and I worked. We had a red phone in Rudy's booth and one on the conducting stand. It was a one-to-one phone. Nobody could hear what Don was saying or what I was saying. Don always had a copy of the arrangement prepared for me so I could follow exactly what's going on. I could say to Don on the phone, "When you get to letter B on the fourth bar, so-and-so is not making it. So take that part out. Also, the violas and the violins are screwing [up] on this part."

Don Sebesky: Creed is an introvert. He would use me as a way to communicate with the musicians. He never actually did. He stayed in the booth. I remember him saying, sotto voce, "Tell J. J. Johnson he's playing a little sharp." That was my job. I had to tell J.J., "Man, can I talk to you for a moment?"

Creed Taylor: I'm not going to waste my goodwill by criticizing J. J. Johnson—not when I've got Don Sebesky, who didn't mind doing it at all.

The CTI album covers themselves were works of art. Taylor used the exotic photography of Pete Turner, who traveled the world for magazines like *Esquire* and provided the producer with striking imagery from Africa, Southeast Asia, and South America that set his jazz records apart from all the others.

Don Sebesky: Creed discovered Pete Turner. He just said, "This is my guy." He said, "Show me what you've got this month." Then he used Pete's photographs. Creed didn't deviate at all. He wanted excellence in aspects of record production: the best musicians, the best photos, the best sound engineer, the best he could get. But it was unified, it had continuity, it has a style like any other artistic endeavor. There was this set of guidelines that we now know to be the Creed Taylor style.

Taylor had his biggest success at A&M with Montgomery's *A Day in the Life*. The guitarist applied his signature technique to pop tunes like the aforementioned Lennon and McCartney song and the Association's "Windy." The string-laden album went gold. But the *Village Voice*'s Gary Giddins lambasted Taylor after Montgomery's tragically premature death in 1968 for failing to capture the guitarist playing straightahead jazz at the height of his powers. "No one twisted Wes Montgomery's arm to make commercial records," the critic wrote. "What is unforgivable is that Creed Taylor didn't respect Montgomery's artistry enough to ensure its preservation." At the same time, however, *A Day in the Life* was wildly popular and brought new listeners to jazz.

Don Sebesky: Wes had an audience before he went with Creed. It was X. When he did "Windy," and it became X times ten, people lined up around the block to see him. He would play "Windy," and then he could do whatever he wanted, Monk, whatever. It brought people in the jazz fold.

The funny thing is, when we first went into the studio to record Wes with strings, we were going to record it all live. We did a couple of takes. Nothing was happening. Wes was clearly uncomfortable. He said, "Man, these cats all went to Julliard. I shouldn't be in the same room with them." You see, he couldn't read music. He was just natural talent, kind of a savant.

Creed Taylor: He'd never been faced with a situation like that. It was an embarrassing thing for him as a musician. There were all these string players sawing away, and he couldn't read a note. Wes sat there with a blank look on his face. So Don made Fender Rhodes tracks of his parts. Wes took them with him on the road, and he learned them. Then we figured it didn't make sense to have a whole bunch of string players in there with Wes. So we just added them later. After that, we didn't do a live date with strings with anyone else. Why did I use strings on so many records? Because I wanted to get them played on the radio. It's as simple as that. It was an uphill battle. You had to get acquainted with the disc jockeys. The Black stations had a jazz show after midnight. If the jazz guys got a reaction to the record, they'd tell the daytime jocks. That's when the records would become a big thing. The strings helped. So did the pop songs.

Taylor wasn't the only guy at A&M who had ideas about blending pop and jazz. Herb Alpert had some too. It wasn't long before Taylor decided it was time to go out on his own.

Creed Taylor: Herb started making suggestions. I told myself, "You gotta get out of this situation." It got to the point where I was being inundated with stuff I didn't approve of. I felt I was wasting too many brain cells trying to get around this situation. He had some idea about the Supremes for this Paul Desmond record. They were very popular at the time. He'd go to the piano in Jerry Moss's office. He'd play four bars of something, then he'd say, "Do you think that would work?" What was I, some third-rate record producer? So I split. Believe me. Herb is not a pushy guy. It wasn't a matter him of him telling me what to do. It was just all this suggesting.

In 1970, Taylor launched CTI as an independent label. Now that he was his own boss, the producer went after the players he'd always wanted to record. First on the list was Stanley Turrentine, the soulful tenor man who would make great records like *Sugar*, *Salt Song*, and *Don't Mess with Mr. T.* for the label. His first date, however, ended up instead being the first release by classically trained jazz flutist Hubert Laws, another soon-to-be CTI star.

Creed Taylor: I had booked a studio in Memphis with Elvis Presley's rhythm section, and it was supposed to be Stanley Turrentine. At ten o'clock in the morning on the day of the date, I get a call from Stanley. He says, "My lawyer won't let me come down, because we didn't sign a contract." So I called Hubert Laws.

Hubert Laws: I had one of the best jobs in New York City for a musician. I was in *The David Frost Show* band led by Billy Taylor. He told us, "I've convinced these television producers that you guys are special. We can't have you coming in and out and getting subs all the time." I took off one time for religious purposes. The second time, Billy said, "I'm sorry, but if you take off again, I can't take you back." But I got this call from Creed, so I went. That was one of the best moves I ever made. That record was *Crying Song*. It was the beginning of my relationship with CTI, which was fantastic.

Next on Taylor's list was Freddie Hubbard. A decade earlier, Taylor produced Oliver Nelson's classic Impulse recording, *The Blues and the Abstract Truth*, and he was blown away by Hubbard's impassioned solo on "Stolen Moments." As soon as he could, he put Hubbard in Van Gelder's studio with saxophonist Joe Henderson, pianist Herbie Hancock, bassist Ron Carter, and drummer Lenny White. The result was *Red Clay*, the seminal jazz-funk album that put Taylor's fledgling label on the map. But to hear the participants tell it, the session was as smooth as you'd guess.

Ron Carter: Freddie came in at the last minute, scuffling. He was still writing the music for the date. It was our job in the rhythm section to make his songs work. Of course, we hadn't even heard the pieces.

(above) Creed with Wes Montgomery. Photo by Chuck Stewart. (below) Wes Montgomery. Photo by Roberto Polillo.

Freddie Hubbard: It was weird. Creed made suggestions. He wanted Herbie to play organ on one song. Herbie had never played organ. Lenny had this steel drum. Herbie didn't like the sound of it.

Creed Taylor: Lenny White did have kind of a strange drum sound; I remember that. I don't know what we did about that. I think we talked to Rudy. We did something. Obviously, the record turned out to be quite good.

Hubbard, Turrentine, Laws, Benson, and Carter quickly became CTI's public faces. They were the label's house band. They recorded their own albums as leaders and played on each other's dates. But behind scenes, Taylor was firmly in control. He picked the lineups for each session.

Creed Taylor: I have my favorite bass players, my favorite drummers. Certain players I wouldn't have together on the same date, but I might have one of them on another date. Well, look, it's like a baseball manager. It's a different aesthetic. But it's similar. You count on your main pitcher to go seven innings. Then you bring in your closer, the guy who's gonna finish the game up. Then you have a shortstop. Maybe he's not hitting that well. So you have the designated hitter. I mean, here's this guy [former Yankees manager] Joe Torre. He's calling all the shots. He knows when he's going to take that pitcher out of the game. Even though on the surface, it bears little resemblance to music in a sense, it's the same thing. It's a team of outstanding players who are out there to win the ball game, and they've got guidance.

Hubert Laws: The guys Creed chose had a special sound. I mean sonically, not so much their concept of playing. All you have to hear is one note, and you know it's Stanley Turrentine. Nobody else had Freddie Hubbard's sounds. Same with George Benson. I thought I was the least of them. I feel I play much better today than I did back then. But Creed chose me to be a part of that. I was honored.

Don Sebesky: And Ron Carter? His sound filled up the entire spectrum of the lower register. That was what was so good about it. He was the cornerstone of the rhythm sections on all these records. You can't go wrong if you have someone like Ron in the rhythm section. No matter who goes out and plays in front of that rhythm section,

they are going to love it.

John Snyder (the label's lawyer who later founded the Horizon jazz series for A&M): A lot people didn't like those records because they were kind of canned. But it was professional record producing at its highest level. It was Creed's vision. It was attention to every detail—he made sure the recording quality was the best in the world, the cover was best in the world. We're not talking second best. We're talking about the best. And he spent money lavishly to achieve it.

Bob James: One of the things I can remember is that Creed and Rudy would not let the records be longer than eighteen minutes on a side. If you went any longer, you have to squeeze the groove. You'd lose bass, and you'd lose quality. Rudy would make the groove wide, which translates into better bass. I really think that's one of the reasons Ron became such a big star. Those CTI records just made him sound so good.

Serious jazz fans had always admired the musicians Taylor signed to CTI. But now that he was producing their records, they had hits on jazz radio.

Freddie Hubbard: Creed got me to Japan. That was a big part of my career. He got me a Grammy for *First Light* [the trumpeter's third CTI record]. So I will always be grateful to him. He was a good producer, and he had nice album covers too. You could do a few so-called funk tunes with Creed. He made me record *The Godfather* theme. He had me do this one thing, "Kicking the Habit" by the Beatles? [It was actually John Lennon's "Cold Turkey" released on the CD version of *Red Clay*.] But they were all hip tunes. He'd say, "Why don't you do some of these songs? You'll sell more records." He had me playing these songs by Bix Beiderbecke. You ever hear "In a Mist?" I had to take that one and practice it. People said, "Why are you doing that?" I said, "'Cause Creed told me to do it."

Taylor had even bigger ambitions. He started a funkier jazz label called Kudu, which became the home of alto saxophonist Hank Crawford, organ player Johnny Hammond Smith, singer Esther Phillips, and a newcomer, saxophonist Grover Washington Jr. The house rhythm section at CTI's sister label was drummer Steve Gadd, guitarist Eric Gale, and keyboard player Richard Tee, who later formed the band Stuff.

Creed with Freddie Hubbard during the recording of *Straight Life*, November 1970. Photo by Chuck Stewart.

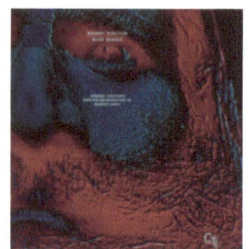 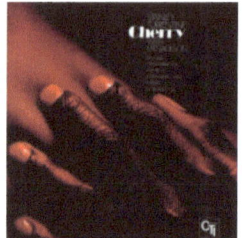  
 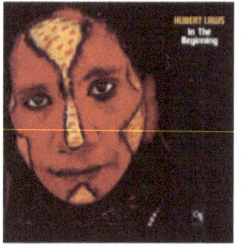 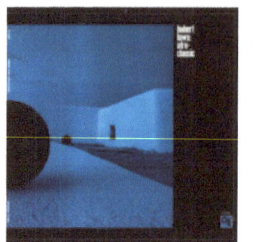 
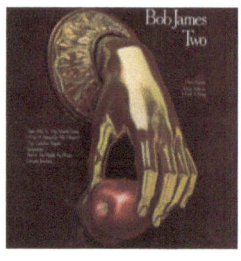   
   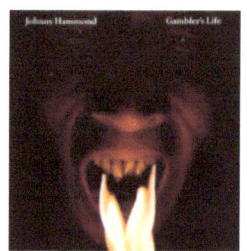
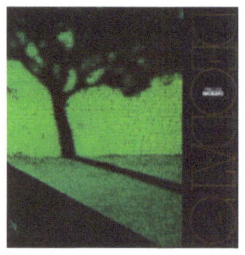   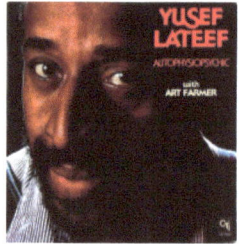

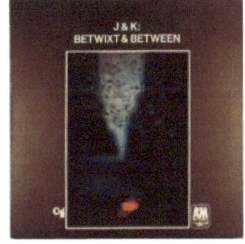

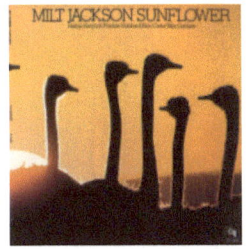

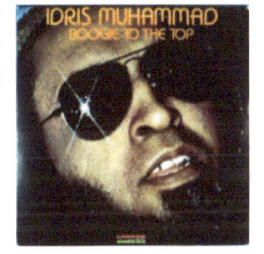

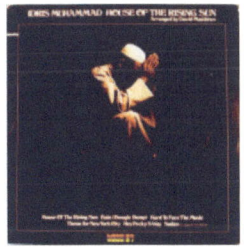

Creed Taylor: The Kudu is an African antelope, right? The color combination [in the logo] is actually Jamaican—the green, black, and red. So that was supposed to be, with apologies, the R&B side of CTI. So we could go into the radio stations and give the guys something they could really get into. Then they would follow some CTI jazz. It was sort of a trade-off, a mix and match.

Bob James: For whatever reason, Creed didn't want all his records to be on CTI. So he started Kudu. It was more African American, even though we weren't using that term then. It was aimed at the R&B audience. So Creed was sticking the funkiest, most R&B-influenced albums over there.

John Snyder: He put those expert groove players in the studio with Hank Crawford. All of a sudden, Hank Crawford was selling two hundred thousand records. Nobody sold as many records as they sold with Creed.

Bob James: I was the arranger on Grover's first session in 1971. I had written all these arrangements, but they weren't for Grover. They were for Hank Crawford. The concept was to have a horn section and do it live. There were three saxes, a trumpet, and trombone. Grover was in the sax section. He had been hired to play tenor. The arrangements were written for Hank playing alto. We all arrived in the studio—everyone but Hank [who was in jail]. Creed was kind of desperate. He just asked Grover to be the lead guy. Grover hadn't brought an alto; I don't remember if he owned one or not.

Creed Taylor: [Hank] was in Memphis. He'd been picked up before for holding marijuana—a terrible drug. [*laughs*] He was a three-time loser. Down South, you can't be Black and be a three-time loser. He coudn't get word to us until 1:00 PM at Rudy's studio. I finally said, "Grover, you have to play Hank's part, because we can't not do this record." So I rented an alto sax, and Grover played it.

Bob James: We were late getting started, but we did the session. That was the project that became *Inner City Blues*. It was a huge record for Grover. Hank Crawford was not particularly happy about that.

John Snyder: Grover was just sitting in the section reading music. Then he sells four hundred thousand copies of his first record. He didn't even know what hit him. All the Kudu records sold like crazy. But the other records did too. George Benson sold well. One hundred fifty thousand, two hundred thousand records. Freddie Hubbard and Stanley Turrentine too.

Hoping to sell even more records, Taylor took his artists on the road, billing them as the CTI All-Stars. The tours yielded several fine live albums, including 1971's *California Concert: The Hollywood Palladium* and the three-part *CTI Summer Jazz at the Hollywood Bowl*, recorded in 1972. For $7.50, audiences could hear Hubbard, Laws, Turrentine, Crawford, and Benson, and their Kudu counterparts, perform their hits backed by James, Carter, Airto, and drummer Jack DeJohnette.

Creed Taylor: The Hollywood Palladium [concert] was a huge sellout. We did the same thing at the Hollywood Bowl. It was a near sellout. I remember, at the last minute, I called up this plane company to drag a banner along a beach on Saturday before the show, and it said "CTI All-Stars Hollywood Bowl Premiering Tonight." And as soon as that plane started flying with the banner, the tickets started selling. We did a lot of stuff like that. We would go to Cincinnati, Chicago, Detroit, Boston, and down South. The CTI band was really an aggregation of the soloists who had their own albums to promote. Each player could play with a large ensemble to more or less replicate his recorded album. If it hadn't been for the large ensemble, it certainly wouldn't have had the same impact.

Ron Carter: The tours? They were great. What always amazed me was, the other jazz labels never picked up on that. Creed took this band on tour to Japan. It's the same band onstage as on the records. I couldn't understand why Blue Note and CBS didn't pick up on this. And just to see all those guys for more than twenty minutes was wonderful.

Hubert Laws: Those tours were very enjoyable for me. That was the first time I went to Japan. They received us like we were rock stars. There were these huge banners saying at the Narita Airport that said: "Welcome CTI All-Stars." It was a great experience. I was always taking photos. We had a great time on those buses. Sometimes, we'd go by train. But it was always high quality, first class.

And the hits, forgive the cliché, kept coming. In 1972, Brazilian pianist-arranger Eumir Deodato's *Prelude* sold five million copies.

Creed driving with Richie Landrum and Weldon Irvine in the backseat, leaving Rudy Van Gelder's studio after a *Cherry* session, May 1972. Photo by Chuck Stewart.

Creed Taylor: I knew ["Also Sprach Zarathustra"] was going to be a hit, but not that big. I figured if Eumir can pull it off so it swings, then we have something really great going, because it's such a universal melody. How can you miss? It wasn't just the arrangement that they got going. It was the Deodato's piano and the other rhythmical components in the studio. We had two bass players, Ron Carter and Stanley Clarke, on that one.

The following year, Washington had his biggest CTI record, *Mister Magic*.

Creed Taylor: Eric Gale was with Roberta Flack at the time. He made this tape of "Mr. Magic" that he had just recorded with Roberta. He gave it to me. He said, "The tune ain't shit, but why don't we give it a try?"

Bob James: I prepared the arrangement. We spent hours going over the groove. I had this little chunky piano-chord rhythm thing and a bass line. Eric added this magic counterpoint guitar line. It just kind of jelled.

Creed Taylor: Bob kept doggedly adding this, going over and over until it finally locked in. It was Harvey Mason, Eric Gale, and Gary King. It was just unbelievable, unbeatable.

Bob James: We were trying to figure out how to cut it, because every time we played it, it was just running long. Creed said, "Once you get the groove going, don't ever stop it." That was a major, major obsession of Creed's. Don't break up the groove. He was so right. Once you get the groove going, you can stay with it forever. So we did. What was it, nine minutes? That was almost unheard of in those days. It would prevent you from getting a single on the radio. But not this time.

Taylor was so smitten with James's work with Washington that he signed the pianist-arranger as a solo artist. The irony is that James had given up long ago on being a leader. He was now intent on being an arranger. Then he recorded *One*, his first CTI album in 1974. That changed everything.

Bob James: In my head, I was thinking of it more as an audition that I could use to get other arranging gigs. I saw it as a one-off thing. So I tried all different kinds of styles—large ensemble, orchestral stuff, arrangements of classical themes like [Mussorgsky's] "Night on Bald Mountain" and Pachelbel's "In the Garden." I didn't think about touring or forming a band or anything. Then two of the pieces on that record, "Night on Bald Mountain" and "Feel Like Making Love" both got a lot of airplay. Within six months, I knew at least there were going to be two albums. At least there was going to be a follow-up. Even then, I was still thinking primarily that the bulk of my work would be as an arranger. I wasn't particularly comfortable playing the melody. I was used to Grover Washington or Hank Crawford or Hubert Laws playing the melody. Then occasionally, I'd play a piano solo. When I look back at those records, it's kind of [like] psychotherapy. I had to kind of build up the confidence to be the lead voice on my own record. I was so much more comfortable being an accompanist. Even then, it was quite a while before I had feedback that people thought I had a style or a sound of my own. I always preferred using the acoustic piano. The Rhodes was so clunky. That was the problem with other piano players. They couldn't change when they played the Rhodes. I had to fight and fight until I found a touch that was different. Here it is thirty years later, and I'm stuck with it.

Taylor was now the most successful producer in the jazz world. He wore expensive clothes and drove a fancy car. Taylor also had an unbelievably plush office in New York City.

Freddie Hubbard: He was in one of those tall buildings in Rockefeller Center. He could push a button and a bar would come out of the wall.
John Snyder: It was all white. He would sit behind this big round table in one of his blue velour suits. I thought he was God.
Hubert Laws: He used to drive a Mercedes. I used to say, "I want to drive a Mercedes like that!"
Don Sebesky: Rockefeller Center was part of the flush era. We had all this money. We figured we might as well spend it. Believe me, I could feel the economic pull. It was the beginning of the end. I think a hit [like Deodato's *Prelude*] goes to anybody's head. You see the world through a different set of glasses.

Taylor was too busy making records to notice. One of the last great records he made was Chet Baker's 1974 album *She Was Too Good to Me*. The James Dean–like trumpet idol from the 1950s had had all his teeth knocked out three years earlier while trying to score heroin. Baker resuscitated his chops. He never entirely kicked his habit. So he was frustratingly uneven after his comeback. Taylor captured some of Baker's most superb playing on *She Was Too Good to Me*, an all-star CTI affair with James on piano, Carter on bass, drummers Jack DeJohnette and Steve Gadd, and arrangements by Sebesky.

John Snyder: There was this guy in Jersey who kept sending me tapes of Chet. He sounded terrible. I was a Chet lover too. He was just not up to it at first. But I felt I heard progress as time went on. I'd give them to Creed. He'd say, "He's lost it." I'd say, "Creed, he's getting better. He's probably going to be okay." Finally, Creed said, "Let's get him some new teeth."
Creed Taylor: He came back better than ever. And with no pressure at all. He had to work to get it. I remember he showed up at the session in a sports car with this girl on his arm. He handed me a tape. He said, "This is my girlfriend. Here's her demo." Then he whispered to me, "She can't sing worth shit."
Don Sebesky: He is one of my musical heroes. It was like a dream come true. He got himself up mentally for the sessions, because he knew he couldn't jive his way through. He was forced to come up to the level of the people around him. He was there ready to play. He wasn't a good communicator. But through his instrument, he was. That's where the background that Creed set up helped. We never had a rehearsal. We just went right into the studio.
Ron Carter: Chet knew we were kind of no-nonsense guys. He had a habit. But he knew we weren't into that. We weren't into that drug zone. He was determined to make his impact as big as ours, even with his habit. He was determined to take care of business. He didn't look for a way out, because there wasn't one.
John Snyder: Chet wasn't bullshitting himself at that time. He wasn't stupid. He rose to the occasion.

Things started to unravel. The CTI All-Stars grew restless. They wanted more control over their records. This led to battles with their domineering producer. Taylor downplays these tensions. But his artists remember things differently.

Freddie Hubbard: He always ended up suggesting certain players on certain records. They were usually pretty good. But I had my own bands then. Creed said, "I want Ron Carter on this. I want George Benson." My guys would say, "Maybe you and Creed should go shove it." He ended up breaking up a lot of my bands. We were making all these records with guys who I'd never play with if it wasn't on the records. I mean, those guys would have wanted a lot of money. [Pianist] Cedar Walton was in my band. I wanted to use Cedar on my record. Creed said no. Milt Jackson was able to use Cedar. But he had to argue a lot to get him.

Hubert Laws: I remember when Freddie Hubbard came into the studio, and he wanted to use the conga player from his group. Creed and Rudy Van Gelder refused to run the recording machines. Freddie wanted him on there, but Creed and Rudy did not. As a result, they would not run the machines. It wasn't a volatile confrontation. They just gave Freddie the silent treatment.

Don Sebesky: Creed protected that aspect of his producing fiercely. That's what made his sound. If you take that way, it's not his record anymore. That's his whole contribution.

John Snyder: Creed knew you are just not going to get the same result with the road band. The musicians didn't like it. They didn't like being cast in Creed's movie. He made them movie stars. But he also made them schizophrenic.

Bob James: All of us musicians were just tools in his achieving what he wanted. He had a monumental ego about that. I wouldn't hesitate to describe it like that. In some ways, the musicians were kind of dismissible and interchangeable, depending on his desire at that moment. It meant nothing to him to say, "No, this conga player is out of here." And he would do it in all kinds of bizarre ways. I remember Creed and Rudy would disappear. They would go to lunch and just not come back if the artist was doing something on his own that didn't relate to what Creed and Rudy wanted to do. That would be it. Session's over.

John Snyder: I think that was a love-hate relationship. Creed is not warm and fuzzy; he's not going to hang out with you and be your friend. The musicians were chattel. Sometimes, the musicians didn't even know what they were going to play or who they were going to play with before the recording sessions. George Benson had issues with that. So did Freddie Hubbard. So did Grover.

Bob James: Grover was frustrated about not being able to use his own musicians. And not being able to make a lot of decisions, creative decisions. In some ways, I was in a very awkward position. I had to try to represent Creed and do what Creed wanted. Creed has very specific ideas about the tunes and the arrangements. Grover wanted to escape. He felt like he was in prison, and I was the prison warden. It really had a not-so-nice impact on our friendship. Creed also insisted that Grover was a sex symbol. He pushed the hell out of that with the album covers where Grover had his shirt off, coming out the swimming pool [on *Mr. Magic*]. Everything was very deliberate stuff. But it was problematic. Grover's wife, Christine, was very involved at that time. That wasn't the image she wanted for him. Grover wanted to be thought of as a serious artist, more like Coltrane. That wasn't his calling. He was a melodic, charismatic, pop type of guy. But he discovered that later.

John Snyder: I remember one time Grover and his wife, Christine, came by the office. Christine said, "He doesn't want to make a record called *Mr. Magic*. He's a serious artist." Creed went into his closet. He got out his velvet coat. He didn't say a word. He just left. Christine and Grover turned to me and said, "What was that all about?" I said, "He made you a millionaire. He's probably insulted. You want to be a serious artist, go ahead." Creed has a way. He knows when something is right.

Well, most of the time. In the midst of all this, Taylor made a terrible business decision. Ultimately, it would be CTI's downfall.

Creed Taylor: The Deodato thing was such a cash cow, let's face it. I had this financial head who said, "Why don't you start your own distribution branch? Why do we need these middle men?" Well, we opened warehouses in Cherry Hill, New Jersey, Dallas, Philly, Canada, California, Washington state, and St. Louis. It was just this ridiculous overexpansion. By the way, when Esther Phillips had her hit, "What a Diff'rence a Day Makes,"

Ron Carter (top) and Hubert Laws during *The Rite of Spring* sessions, June 1971.
Photos by Chuck Stewart.

everybody thought she should have a gift, a fur coat to show our appreciation. [My financial advisor] Herman said, "Give her one that's three-quarter length with a zipper or buttons. Don't give her the second part until she gets another hit."

Bob James: He never stopped making records. He just kept going. He just had this overhead that was getting bigger and bigger and bigger. I watched him just not have any trust for anybody else. He wanted to take more and more control for himself, which was consistent with his recording style and his musical approach. The worst decision was his choice to do his own distribution. He had these offices in all those major cities. Every one of them had all this overhead. I was recording with Creed at the time. He was in the studio all day long. He wasn't supervising the business. Nobody was. There was a lot of corporate people [who] were spending all kinds of money in crazy ways that didn't help sell CTI records. Before you knew it, it mushroomed into this situation where he had this huge debt that he couldn't repay.

Don Sebsesky: I just think he had that hit with Deodato [and] he was under enormous pressure. That changed the dynamic at CTI. It became a different animal after that.

Creed Taylor: We had cash flow from the Deodato record. But when that ran through the pipeline, there was nothing else to fill it. We weren't distributing anybody else's records but ours.

Bob James: It became worse and worse and worse. You had musicians not getting paid. It was really, really bad at the end. I had musicians who had played on my records. They said, "Bob, I'm really happy for you, but I haven't gotten paid." I heard the story from one musician after another. Creed didn't have any money. I felt like he really naively believed that it would all catch up and he'd be able to pay everybody eventually. It didn't happen. Many of us were forced to take him to court.

Freddie Hubbard: We'd go to cash the checks, and they wouldn't clear. He got his money. But we weren't getting paid.

Inevitably, the label's stars departed. Washington and Benson left for Warner Brothers. Hubbard, James, and Laws went to Columbia.

Bob James: What we were doing at CTI was a whole new genre of music. The sales figures were obvious. They were gold in the case of *Mr. Magic*. Some other records were selling well in excess of one hundred thousand units. The major labels suddenly saw these jazz artists like me or Grover or Hubert Laws having much more commercial potential than we would have five years before. Creed made something far bigger than the way jazz was perceived at that time. I was the beneficiary along with all the rest of us. Hubert Laws, Freddie Hubbard… The people at CBS were very aware of it. Bruce Lundvall was very aware of it. Bruce made me a great offer to come to CBS.

Hubert Laws: I never knew musicians could get that kind of money. I had record companies courting me. I couldn't believe some of those companies would make those kinds of offers. I didn't think they could follow through on them. I stayed with him as long as I could. Creed made me an offer. But CBS was offering me this huge signing fee. I just knew it would be a strain for Creed. They were signing us for the kind of money they offered rock stars.

John Snyder: When everybody was going to leave, they would call me and say I need this amount of money. I would tell Creed, but he wouldn't even pick up the phone. He said, "If Freddie Hubbard doesn't know what I did for him, fuck him." I didn't tell Freddie that.

Creed Taylor: That's not true. I never said that. Look, here's what happened with Columbia. Bruce Lundvall [then head of Columbia's jazz division] came to my office. This was right after CTI had won best jazz company of the year from *Billboard*. He wanted to distribute us. Obviously, it was an embarrassment to the majors to have some independent upstart come along and become number one when they had all the financial facility and personnel under the sun. I said, "No thanks, Bruce. I prefer the route we are going." I didn't want to be encumbered by a big corporation. So Columbia decided to set things up to make it difficult for CTI. They were going to try to bring pressure to CTI to become part of Columbia.

In hindsight, perhaps Taylor should have taken the offer. In 1978, CTI filed for bankruptcy. In order to stay in business, he was forced to cut a distribution deal with Columbia. The big label got to distribute Taylor's label. This, of course, means Columbia got a big cut of every CTI record sold. Columbia also loaned CTI $600,000. The catch: Taylor had

Creed Taylor and the demise of CTI, circa late 1970s/early 1980s. Photo by Chuck Stewart.

to pledge his catalog as collateral. A record he produced by Patti Austin sold badly. CTI missed a loan payment. The producer lost everything.

> **Creed Taylor:** The chairman of the board of trustees for the bankruptcy court [overseeing the CTI case] happened to be the attorney for Columbia. He is the guy who negotiated the deal. They knew what steps they had to take after that to get what they wanted.
>
> **John Snyder:** It was a mess. It all came down to the fact that he put those masters up as security. Columbia foreclosed.

Columbia and Warner tried hard to copy the CTI formula with Taylor's former artists. George Benson went on to become one of the biggest names in pop at Warner. But overall, these new records weren't as good as the ones that Taylor himself had produced.

> **Hubert Laws:** They thought they could get the same sound if they used the same studio. I know Bob tried to record with Rudy Van Gelder. I recorded a couple of my things over there when I went to CBS. But Creed was an important element in bringing things together. He would always say if something was overarranged. If there were too many instruments playing, he'd cut out the fat. That was his signature.
>
> **John Snyder:** It was Creed. Those other guys just didn't have everything right. It's the guy. It's him. You can't replicate that. I got hired by A&M after that. They thought I could do the same thing. But I wanted to make records that were representative of the artist. I got fired after two years. The art of making a record is not just putting up a mic in front of a group of guys who make music together. It's not capturing something. It's creating something. Records are illusion. They are like movies. When you go to [see] *Batman*, you know it's not really happening. But you buy into it. You say this is a rational universe. That's what Creed did. He made it look like the rabbit was really coming out of the hat. That's not something anybody is born doing. I don't know of anybody who did it better than Creed—whether you like it or not.
>
> **Bob James:** I don't think the idea of money or commercial success was uppermost in Creed's mind. I just think he loved being in the studio. He had a huge ego and expensive tastes. But as far as his approach to music, it was much more pure.

The irony is that when Taylor tried to stage a comeback by making blatantly commercial records in the '90s, he failed miserably. Once, he could get his music played on the radio. Now, it was no longer so easy.

> **Creed Taylor:** This was about the time [radio station] CD-101 was getting really hot. You know, GRP was making all that garbage saxophone stuff. I decided, "Well, if you can't beat 'em, join 'em." I made some really unwise decisions just from production, music sampling, trying to squeeze music into their format, because they had become so omnipotent.
>
> **Don Sebesky:** They [had] strict guidelines at CD-101. They gave Creed a whole laundry list. But you have to have freedom. That was the essence of what Creed was all about.
>
> **Creed Taylor:** It obviously didn't work out.

Today, the producer runs a website where he sells CTI CDs reissued by Sony, the Japanese conglomerate that now owns Columbia. This must be painful for Taylor. The CDs include outtakes that he would have never released. The liner notes barely acknowledge his contributions. Still, the great producer dreams of one last return to the studio. He and Sebesky are trying to reunite the surviving CTI All-Stars to record an album and tour Europe.

> **Creed Taylor:** We had a dynamite band lined up including Airto and Pachito. The rhythm section would just be killing. But the European concert promoters were trying to get into the act. They wanted to book the CTI band, but they wanted to see all dead or alive members back in the CTI band. Of course, the economy isn't helping. Things change though.
>
> **Ron Carter:** Tell Creed to give me a call. My price has gone up since then. But I'm available.
>
> **Don Sebesky:** We're going to go back and do it just like we used to—the same format, the same outlook, the same standard of excellence that Creed stood for. That's what really made CTI so great.
>
> **Hubert Laws:** I've been talking to Creed about this. I hope it happens. For me, it's not even the money. I'd just do it for the sake of the music. ●

RICKY-TICK RECORDS PRESENTS...

The Five Corners Quintet: "Hot Corner" CD/LP
"Without dumbing down or selling out they have moved jazz out of the dark ages" -The Observer. Released in March 2009.

Jukka Eskola: "Jova" / "Chip 'n' Charge" single
"One of the most talented trumpeters of his generation" - Jazzwise

The Five Corners Quintet: "Othello" EP
Jazzical Twist of the Scaffold

Povo: "On the Spot Reworks" EP
Ten nu-jazzers interpret Scand jazz greats

Distributed by Wax Poetics www.waxpoetics.com   www.ricky-tick.com

MEMPHIS SOUL!

The City Champs "The Safecracker"
ER 103 LP/CD/DIGITAL

"The Safecracker" features 7 prime cuts of Stax/Hi Records, Prestige and Blue Note inspired soul-jazz and funk from Memphis' premier organ trio-The City Champs. The sessions were tracked and mixed entirely on analog tape—a Scully 1" 8-track machine, which was the same model used at Stax, Muscle Shoals Sound, and Chip Moman's American Studio. Mastered by Larry Nix at Ardent Studios on the mastering lathe he used daily at Stax

Available online and in-stores on March 17, 2009

The Bo-Keys feat. Harvey Scales "Work That Skirt" b/w "Cracker Jack"
ER 104 45RPM (w/ pic. sleeve)/DIGITAL

The Bo-Keys team up with Stax/Chess/Magic Touch/Casablanca recording artist, Harvey Scales, to bring you the Summer's hottest hit - "Work That Skirt". The B-Side features a slinky instrumental soul groover - "Cracker Jack". Strictly limited to 500 copies.

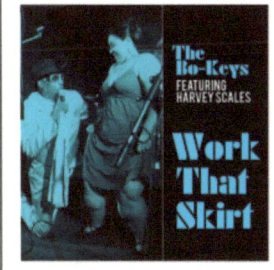

Available April 7, 2009 - taking pre-orders now

777 S. MAIN ST, MEMPHIS, TN 38106 • WWW.ELECTRAPHONICRECORDING.COM

BUY, SELL & TRADE FROM DC'S BEST SELECTION OF NEW & USED VINYL

SOM Records

1843 14TH STREET NW
WASHINGTON, DC 20009
202.328.3345

OPEN DAILY NOON 'TIL LATE!
WWW.SOMRECORDSDC.COM

KING UNDERGROUND.COM

The Hip Hop Specialists

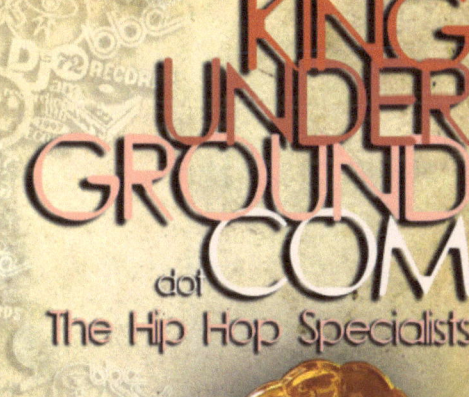

UK, US & Rare Hip Hop Vinyl, Turntablist tools, CD's DVD's & Clothing

Special offers & free stickers with all orders.

EL MICHELS AFFAIR
ENTER THE 37TH CHAMBER

Brooklyn's leading purveyors of cinematic soul offer
live reinterpretations of Wu-Tang Clan's finest instrumentals

Includes "C.R.E.A.M.", "Bring Da Ruckus", "Protect Ya Neck", "Can It All Be So Simple," and many more

MUSIC INSPIRED BY THE
WU-TANG

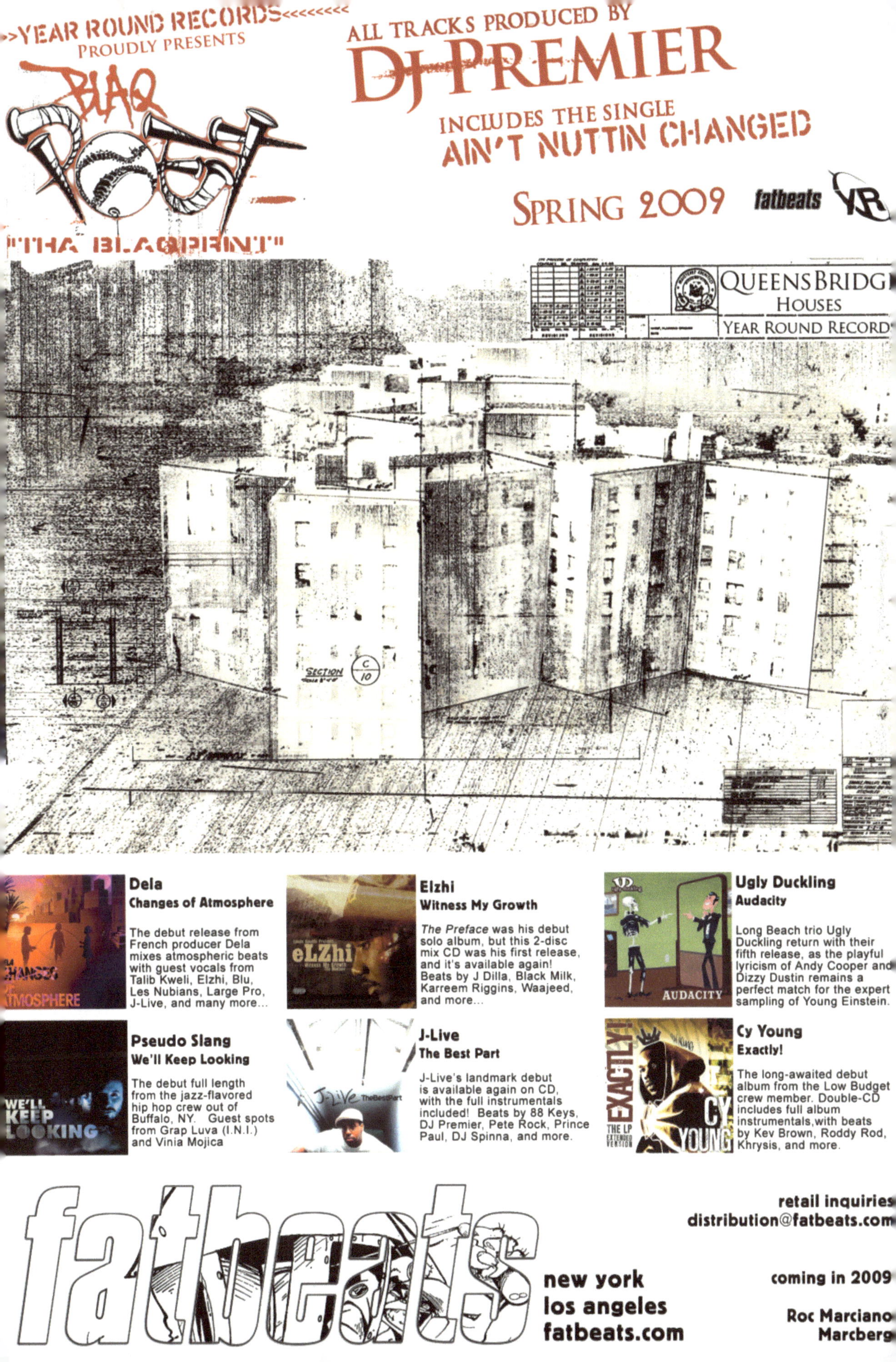

YEAR ROUND RECORDS
PROUDLY PRESENTS

BLAQ POET
"THA BLAQPRINT"

ALL TRACKS PRODUCED BY DJ PREMIER

INCLUDES THE SINGLE
AIN'T NUTTIN CHANGED

SPRING 2009   fatbeats

QUEENSBRIDGE HOUSES
YEAR ROUND RECORD

Dela
Changes of Atmosphere

The debut release from French producer Dela mixes atmospheric beats with guest vocals from Talib Kweli, Elzhi, Blu, Les Nubians, Large Pro, J-Live, and many more...

Elzhi
Witness My Growth

The Preface was his debut solo album, but this 2-disc mix CD was his first release, and it's available again! Beats by J Dilla, Black Milk, Karreem Riggins, Waajeed, and more...

Ugly Duckling
Audacity

Long Beach trio Ugly Duckling return with their fifth release, as the playful lyricism of Andy Cooper and Dizzy Dustin remains a perfect match for the expert sampling of Young Einstein.

Pseudo Slang
We'll Keep Looking

The debut full length from the jazz-flavored hip hop crew out of Buffalo, NY. Guest spots from Grap Luva (I.N.I.) and Vinia Mojica.

J-Live
The Best Part

J-Live's landmark debut is available again on CD, with the full instrumentals included! Beats by 88 Keys, DJ Premier, Pete Rock, Prince Paul, DJ Spinna, and more.

Cy Young
Exactly!

The long-awaited debut album from the Low Budget crew member. Double-CD includes full album instrumentals, with beats by Kev Brown, Roddy Rod, Khrysis, and more.

fatbeats

new york
los angeles
fatbeats.com

retail inquiries
distribution@fatbeats.com

coming in 2009

Roc Marciano
Marcberg

The SECOND COMING of HIP

Producer Joel Dorn helmed a funky golden era for Atlantic
text **John Kruth**

There's an old swing tune with a lyric that goes, "Some cats know." Record producer Joel Dorn knew in a big way. "Joel talked in jazz, walked in jazz, and thought in jazz," doo-wop legend Dion DiMucci told me shortly after J.D. died in 2007. Dion nailed it, but that's only part of the story—there was his love of classic comedy, (W. C. Fields, Laurel and Hardy, Three Stooges, etc.), surrealism (Fellini and Magritte were among his faves), basketball, photography, and cop shows.

Back in the late '60s and early '70s, I used to buy records on the Atlantic label by artists I'd never heard of, simply because Dorn's name appeared on the back of the jacket. His pedigree was flawless. The artists he steered included Roberta Flack, Max Roach, Herbie Mann, Les McCann and Eddie Harris, Bette Midler, Mose Allison, Rahsaan Roland Kirk, Yusef Lateef, Leon Redbone, and the Neville Brothers, to name a few. Dorn himself, I would discover years later, was just as singular as any of them and seriously funny—Larry David funny. Joel died of a heart attack on Monday, December 17, 2007, in New York, punching a hole in the lives of his family and friends about the size of your average airplane hangar, and just as cold and drafty. He was sixty-five.

At the time of his death, Dorn had just completed compiling a box set of Atlantic's greatest jazz sides for Rhino Records called *Hommage à Nesuhi*, dedicated to his mentor, the late, great Nesuhi Ertegun. Joel was a great mentor himself—to producers like Hal Willner, Michael Cuscuna, his son Adam Dorn (aka Mocean Worker), and myself as well, who he generously allowed to coproduce a couple of posthumous Rahsaan Roland Kirk discs.

This interview took place in late October 2007. A visit from Dorn usually lasted in the vicinity of fifteen to twenty minutes before he'd suddenly stand up and announce, "Now, if you'll excuse me, I'm off to help others," as he'd head for the door. This time was different. I'd interviewed Joel a dozen times since 1997, and never had he been so eager to talk and so diligent about details. The tape rolled for nearly three hours. I don't think he even asked for a glass of water the whole time. Something was up, but I hadn't a clue. After he split, my sweetheart Marilyn asked, "What, does he think he's gonna die or something?" Dorn die? The dude looked like he could break you in two. It's a shame he couldn't have stuck around till the end of '08 to see his hometown Phillies and a Black man take all in the same year. His passing is a great loss to American music and culture.

Joel Dorn, 1942–2007. Photo by Faye Rosendorn.

How did you get into music in the first place?
I always loved music. During World War II, my mother used to play me Al Jolson records when I was a year and a half old. "April Showers" used to make me cry. It just tore me apart. I was always into music and always knew I would be in music. I always knew I would never have a real job. I knew that by the time I was seven. But I can't play an instrument. I can't sing. I can't dance. I'm terrible with equipment, so I can't be an engineer. I'm not an arranger. I don't have any skills, but I do have abilities. When I was in junior high, I found out there were guys called A&R [Artist & Repertoire] men who supervised the making of records. They weren't even called producers at that point. I figured if there was any shot for me in the music business, it's the only shot I had. I dug Atlantic. It had a sound, but not like at the label, so I turned over an Atlantic jazz album, and it said "Supervision: Nesuhi Ertegun." So I wrote to him. It was March of '58. I said, "I'm a big fan of Atlantic, and Ray Charles is the best thing I've ever heard," and I asked if I could buy any of his old records direct from the label, as I couldn't find them at the stores. Additionally, I said that someday I'd like to be an A&R man and work at Atlantic. And I gave him an idea for Ray Charles. There was a Gershwin revival going on at the time with the movie *Porgy and Bess*. So I suggested that Atlantic do a version of *Porgy and Bess* with Ray Charles, Clyde McPhatter, Joe Turner, LaVern Baker, and the Drifters. I didn't hear back from him until the end of November that year. It was one of the few times I was comin' home from school in the daylight, as I was usually in detention. My mother was in front of the house,

"My theme song was "Hard Times" by David "Fathead" Newman. And every fourth or fifth record I played was by Atlantic, because I liked 'em."

Motown or Memphis. It had more of an approach. I loved Joe Turner, LaVern Baker, and Chuck Willis, the early Drifters and the Coasters, stuff like that.

Wasn't Ray Charles your main man?
In March of '58, I was sitting in my grandmother's kitchen, listening to "Georgie Woods, the Man with the Goods on WDAS-AM 1480 on your dial," and at nine fifteen on that Friday night, he played a record by a singer I never heard of. It was called "Ain't That Love," and the singer was Ray Charles. And I just lost it. It felt like the planet put its brakes on, stopped, and then started up again. In terms of the turnpike of my life, when I took that exit, I never came back again. I went lookin' for Ray Charles records, and I couldn't find 'em in the White shops in the suburbs. So I went to the Black neighborhoods at Treegoob's at Forty-first and Lancaster in West Philadelphia, or Paramount, one of the few Black-owned shops in the city, on South Street in South Philly. They all knew about Ray Charles, but he hadn't crossed over yet. Not even remotely. They didn't have any of his singles and couldn't get me the old singles. They had an album, part of a rock-and-roll series with Joe Turner and LaVern Baker and Clyde McPhatter. It had a generic cover without any credits on it. I wanted to write somebody wavin' a white piece of paper, sayin' "that man in New York answered you." And it was a letter from Nesuhi.

Sounds like a scene from a Frank Capra movie.
Yeah. So I was in touch with Nesuhi by the time I was fifteen and started to correspond with him. The fact that he wrote back to me six months later and said he thought it was a great idea… Ray Charles was my life! So he put me on their mailing list, sent me records, and he was really kind. In '61, I was a junior [at Temple University] majoring in communications when I went on the air on WHAT-FM, which was the other Black station in Philly at the time. They hired me as a folk-music disc jockey on the weekends. I didn't know anything about folk music, but I knew a chick who was a left-wing nut, and she put the music together for me. They'd let me play jazz for an hour. Then I got a full-time slot. So now I'm nineteen and a full-time jazz disc jockey. Right away, I was Atlantic's best friend, jazz-wise, in the known universe. My theme song was "Hard Times" by David "Fathead" Newman. And every fourth or fifth record I played was by Atlantic, because I liked 'em. I would never compromise the show. I loved Atlantic, Blue Note, Prestige, Riverside… Fathead had made his first album as a leader. It was called *Fathead: Ray Charles Presents David Newman*,

Ray Charles. Photo by Leni Sinclair.

and it was doin' okay as a jazz album, but it didn't really bust out. When I made it my theme song, it started sellin' hundreds of copies a month in Philly. So that refocused my connection with Nesuhi. I was also a jazz disc jockey that could pick a track. Atlantic would send me all their stuff prior to its release date, and I would tell them "this is the track," or "there is no track," or "this will get some play, but it won't sell." I knew how to do that. It wasn't an esoteric jazz show just for jazz heads. It was a good-time jazz show. I played music that people would really dig, and I got a national reputation as a guy who could sell records.

Did Nesuhi invite you to any sessions around that time, so you could learn how to make records?

Yeah. I had been to sessions that he ran with Betty Carter, Hank Crawford, and Herbie Mann. I watched what he did.

I would drive up to Atlantic sometimes just as a friend, to meet the sales and the promotion people. [Jerry] Wexler or Ahmet [Ertegun] or Tommy [Dowd] would be in the studio. So I started to get my education. I apprenticed to Nesuhi in the old way, like he was a shoemaker. I'd observe him, and he'd let me try things. He finally took a shot on me in '63. I was twenty-two.

How did Nesuhi run the show? Was he a hands-on producer?

He made documentaries. He was more of a capturer. He put his money on talent and captured what they did. He wasn't one of these guys who said, "Let's do a Broadway album, and I'll give you a big drum sound." He wasn't like that.

Nesuhi had impeccable taste.

You gotta remember, he signed Trane, Mingus, and MJQ

at the precise time. Ornette, Herbie Mann, Chris Connor. He took Hank Crawford and Fathead out of the Ray Charles band. He got Mose Allison at his peak. Nesuhi not only had exquisite taste, but he had the ability to pick people at the perfect time. He was on the scene. I think the Atlantic jazz catalog had two golden periods. I might be accused of hubris here. When Nesuhi had it, it was *the* golden period. There was a lull, and then he gave it to me. Mine was the second golden period. His golden period had more gold in it than mine but not necessarily more commercial success.

What kind of deal did Atlantic make with you?
Nesuhi said, "Here, you have fifteen hundred dollars; here's what I want you to do. I want you to find an artist that has never recorded before as a leader. I want you to make the record." The budget included my front money, which was fifty bucks, their front money, which was five hundred dollars, and I had to pay for the studio and the musicians. I used to go to the clubs every night in Philly—Peps, the Showboat. I was underage at the time, but I was friends with the guys that owned the clubs, so they let me come in as long as I didn't drink or make a scene. They were cool, 'cause I'd interview whoever was comin' to town and plug their gig. So I got to see everybody in the clubs when I was nineteen—whoever came through—Miles, Trane, Blakey, Horace [Silver], Eddie "Lockjaw" Davis, Cannon[ball Adderly], Mongo Santamaria, Rahsaan [Roland Kirk], Yusef [Lateef], Sonnny Stitt, Groove Holmes, Shirley Scott and Stanley Turrentine, Lou Rawls, Les McCann, and Eddie Harris.

Sounds like quite a scene.
I had a real feel for what they did. I told [Pep's owner] Jack Goldenberg that I had a shot at Atlantic and had to find somebody that's never recorded. He called me at the station one night and said, "Come down, I got your guy." He had Mongo Santamaria in that week. He said, "There's a kid in his band that's phenomenal." As I walked in, Hubert Laws was taking his solo on "Manha de Carnival." I never heard anybody play flute like that in my life. So I started chasin' him. He was gonna be my ticket in. I told Nesuhi that I found my guy. He said, "Are you *sure*?" And I said, "Yeah." So he said, "Go ahead." I made a record with Hubert Laws called *The Laws of Jazz*. I signed him out of Mongo's band. It was Chick Corea on piano [and] Richard Davis on bass… and the record sold. It wasn't a smash, but it made its money back and more. It sold about five or six thousand copies, which was a big jazz record in those days.

Hubert played some killer flute on "Let Her Go."
That's a piccolo, and he plays the fuck out of it! Chick Corea's playin' Latin piano. Chick came out of Mongo's band; he can really play a montuno. Do you know who's playin' bass? This will blow you away! Cachao! Listen to that groove. I actually recorded Cachao one time.

How many sessions did it take to make the album? Did you cut it on a two-track?
It took two days. We cut it in two three-hour sessions with a day to mix it. Atlantic had the only eight-track machine in the country at the time, thanks to Tommy Dowd. Then Hubert won the best miscellaneous instrument category in the *Down Beat* poll that year, and Herbie Slotkin, who owned Treegoob's Records in West Philly said, "The Hubert Laws record is selling; it seems like you got a touch. You wanna make some records?" So he funded an independent label, which Atlantic put out. And I recorded Sonny Stitt, Duke Pearson, Junior Mance, Joe Zawinul, Robin Kenyatta, and Byard Lancaster. I also signed Fathead, and he drove up from Dallas, and we made *House of David* on a Saturday night. When that came out, it did pretty well. The records were selling, but they weren't doing anything special, like, two thousand copies, and I was playing 'em, like, every thirteen seconds. I completely lost my sense of integrity and control. And then I signed Rufus Harley.

The Black vegetarian jazz bagpiper. They only made one of him.
Yeah. Rufus sold, like, five thousand copies the first month. A disc jockey in Detroit named Ed Love busted it out. So Nesuhi called me in May of '67 and said, "Come to New York." I thought I was gettin' canned. We sat down. I'm not a nervous guy, but I was afraid that my dream had *almost* come true, that I wanted to produce at Atlantic, and I actually got the chance, and I blew it. I was scared. I even put on a tie. Then he said, "Listen, I'd like you to come here and work full-time and be our jazz producer." It hit me double, 'cause I thought I was about to get canned, but now my ship's comin' in.

Nesuhi seemed like a visionary on a lot of levels.
He was a brilliant guy. He had the best combination of eye and ear of anybody I'd ever met. He also had a thundering lack of ego. As brilliant as he was, it was odd to have that kind of vision and to act on passion the way he could, and, at the same time, he was relatively egoless. He wasn't a man who didn't realize who he was, but he didn't have a need to let you know about it or have the world come to him so he could pontificate or bask in his own sunshine. He said, "My time as a record producer is basically over. I'll still do

projects from time to time with my friends, John Lewis and Herbie Mann, but I'm not in the clubs. I'm not in the scene anymore." He said, "This is your time. You're in the clubs." Atlantic was growing, and he was beginning to take care of all their international business. He took Atlantic worldwide, and he did it brilliantly. So he told me, "Remember, if you fail, I gotta let you go. No matter what, we'll still be friends, but you're gonna live or die by what you do." What a way to hire somebody, and what a way to turn the wheel over to somebody.

He obviously saw your ambition and that you cut some good records that actually sold some copies, so he was willing to give you the shot.

Now, I've got high blood pressure and a deviated septum, but I'm not being treated for false humility. I was an okay producer with training wheels that made listenable jazz records. I had good engineers and a good studio with people who knew way more than I did. I had a good eye for talent, and I think he recognized that. I think what he bet on was my ability to bring people to the label the same way that he did. He discovered [arranger/producer] Arif [Mardin]. He brought [photographer] Lee Friedlander in. He brought Leiber and Stoller in, along with Coltrane and Mingus and MJQ.

Let's talk about the box set you're currently working on [entitled Hommage à Nesuhi**]. What were your criteria in selecting the tracks?**

This is a view of what I think was Atlantic jazz in its ascendancy, from when Nesuhi caught his groove in '56 and made that whole run—Trane, Mingus, Ornette, MJQ, Ray Charles, Herbie Mann, Chris Connor, Fathead, Hank… And then he stopped around '62 or '63 and kind of turned it over to Arif. Arif was a big bebop head. He made terrific albums with MJQ and Hank Crawford, but he didn't bring anybody new to the label. Nesuhi let me learn on the job, with company bread. That's a big dice roll. He was no easy act to follow. I'm a great low man on a spectacular totem pole. That wasn't a totem pole that was easy to get on, but I am the low man. And don't forget, when Nesuhi was doing all of this, he was collecting Magritte when for a few thousand dollars you could buy a Magritte painting that sells for about fifteen million now. All of the musicians that he signed would have made music without him, but it wouldn't have been the same as it was on his watch, because he signed geniuses at the right time, and then he set up the best possible situation for them to do what it is they did best.

What were the budgets like on the first jazz records you made?

Well, with Hubert Laws, we had fifteen hundred dollars. Then for the next one, we had twenty-five hundred, so I could add another instrument or extra session. They were jazz budgets. So if you sold a little bit, you could maybe get up to five thousand dollars.

What did you make for cutting a Rahsaan or Yusef record?

By that time, I was already working for the label, so I had a salary. Starting on June 19, 1967, I was making two hundred and fifty dollars a week. I was commuting every day, taking the train up from Philly to New York and back again. When I had sessions at night, I stayed at a cheap hotel for seven dollars a night, where all the stewardesses stayed.

I don't wanna know, Joel…

I think Nesuhi thought it was more economically feasible to let me do what I wanted and either make it or not make it than to go along a step at a time, making jazz records that sold two or three thousand copies. He always told me that when you sign artists, sign people you're willing to do two or three albums with, because sometimes the first one doesn't work, and it's nobody's fault. They have to find themselves or we have to direct them. He also told me, "Never take a musician's publishing, because sometimes that's the only thing they have to live on."

Wow, a guy with integrity. That's a long way from how business is done these days.

When I first got there, I wanted to do a string album with Fathead. In those days, an artist did a string album after they had, like, five successful records. I had Bill Fischer, who I'd used with Joe Zawinul, and I thought that Fathead could be a commercial success. So he let me. It was, like, an eight- or ten-thousand-dollar album with strings. The engineer saved my ass on that one.

Les McCann's records on Limelight had some good stuff on them, but he didn't really break through until he was on Atlantic.

He didn't like the studio. People would stop him and say, "Take two." Or he'd be in the middle of something, and they'd run out of tape. But I knew how to record him. I cut the basic sessions with his trio, and then I overdubbed some Latin percussion with Willie Bobo and Victor Pantoja. And then I had Bill Fischer write the strings. That was *Much Les*, which had "With These Hands," which became a hit. You gotta understand, guys like Creed Taylor would get big budgets to do string albums with Stan Getz or Astrud Gilberto, jazz that crossed over. But Nesuhi let me do two string albums the first two or three months I was there.

Ahmet was obviously a very powerful guy as well.
He was the Babe Ruth of record execs. And [Jerry] Wexler was his Tonto. But the Lone Ranger didn't work without Tonto. Nesuhi and Ahmet had two gigantic personalities. They were two fill-the-room kind of guys. But Nesuhi filled the room with his quietness. In the beginning, I didn't get it. I thought he was the third partner because Ahmet and Jerry cut all the hits while Nesuhi handled the international licensing and the covers. But those covers changed covers. When you'd get a James Brown album or a "5" Royales album in the mid-'50s on King, James Brown would be wearin' an orange suit, and the lettering would be in gold and green. It was insulting shit that they laid on Black audiences, as if they couldn't appreciate anything but bright colors and

Fabric come from?
Nesuhi had a worldview. He always had a global outlook. He was a world citizen, so he brought in Bent Fabric and [clarinetist] Acker Bilk, and they sold like crazy to squares. "The Alley Cat" was a big hit, and Nesuhi brought that in. Nesuhi also brought in ska from Jamaica in the early '60s. He just missed reggae. I was in England, and people were goin' nuts to what sounded to me like roller-skating music with that reverse rhythm. So I called Atlantic, but Wexler nixed it, because we got killed with ska, so Chris Blackwell [of Island Records] grabbed it.

So you had some jazz hits with Les McCann and Eddie Harris. How did you cross over to pop?
We were doin' well with Les. He had already discovered Lou Rawls and Gene McDaniels. Then he called me up one day

"When I called Nesuhi and told him I wanted to sign Roberta Flack, I hadn't even heard her yet. We sent the papers down to her in D.C. before I'd heard her for the first time."

lots of beads. Nesuhi had photos of LaVern Baker and Joe Turner taken by this young photographer, Lee Friedlander, with graphic design by Marvin Israel. It made you buy the records, even if you didn't like them.

Of course. But what Atlantic albums didn't you like?
Oh, there were a few. I had a T-Bone Walker and a Champion Jack Dupree [record] that didn't do it for me at the time. But those covers were stunning. Blue Note was the other label that had a real fastball with those Reid Miles covers with Frank Wolff's photographs. I thought Creed [Taylor] did a great job initially with Verve. So Nesuhi established the Atlantic look, which, I think, was the most singular look.

Nesuhi was obviously a class human being. I went to see his collection of surrealist paintings a few years back at the Guggenheim and was completely knocked out.
He was onto Magritte when all the art critics said he was nothing but an illustrator. When Magritte died in the late '60s, Nesuhi went to Europe and bought thirty oils from his wife, Georgette. They were about ten thousand apiece. Ahmet got ten, Jerry got ten, and Nesuhi got ten. You can't touch a Magritte oil these days for under a couple of million.

Speaking of surrealism, where did pianist Bent

at seven in the morning and said, "I found your next girl singer. Just do what I'm tellin' you and sign her." When I called Nesuhi and told him I wanted to sign Roberta Flack, I hadn't even heard her yet. We sent the papers down to her in D.C. before I'd heard her for the first time. I went to see her in an empty club, and she was spectacular, but I had no idea she was gonna be big. I knew she was good; the quality was there. This is a good example of how Nesuhi let me operate. He said, "Well, if Les really loves her that much, then go sign her. You have ten thousand dollars to make the record." She wanted to record with her own group. Her demo tape wasn't so good; there wasn't anything happening there. But what I saw in the club really worked. I recorded her with her band, but the record wasn't what it could be. I went back to Nesuhi. He'd let me sign someone I never heard based on what Les said. I cut the record, but it didn't work. Now what do I do? I said, "I could really get her if I used my guys." He said, "Okay, record her with your guys." It was unbelievable, unprecedented. So I got Ron Carter, Bucky Pizzarelli, and [drummer] Ray Lucas with Bill Fischer to write the strings. Then we caught a good break with Clint Eastwood where he put it in the movie [*Play Misty for Me*]. Four million singles and two million albums and record of the year for "First

President of Atlantic Records, Nesuhi Ertegun (middle), with vice presidents Jerry Wexler (left) and Ahmet Ertegun (right). Photograph: Michael Ochs Archive/Getty Images.

Time I Ever Saw Your Face" with a Grammy later…
Was it generosity of spirit, intuition, or voodoo?
There was something about Nesuhi that knew when to roll the dice and when not to.
Your production ideas on records like Rahsaan's *The Case of the 3 Sided Dream in Audio Color* and Yusef's *The Doctor Is In and Out* was the bridge between jazz and psychedelia. Those albums had an incredible atmosphere and sounds never heard before on jazz records.
Even though my heroes were Leiber and Stoller, [Phil] Spector, and George Martin, I was just as influenced by the painters that Nesuhi turned me on to, as well as film directors like Fellini and Bergman. People might wonder what the hell I was doin', but then one of them might sell two hundred thousand copies, and it made up for the three that were nuts. He let me do what I wanted, and I'm eternally grateful for letting my dream come true. Look, one day I was buyin' records by Ray Charles in May, and then I'm at the place where Ray made his records in September. Workin' for Atlantic was like playin' for the '55 Dodgers. This may sound like opinion, but as far as I'm concerned, Atlantic was the greatest record company ever—period.
Blue Note and Verve never had that kind of diversity. Columbia had some great stuff but…
If we had pop, it was hip pop. If we had R&B, it was hip R&B. If we had jazz, it was hip jazz. When we put out square music, like Acker Bilk, we put out the best square music. Stuff like "Stranger on the Shore" was a gigantic record.

That could have been enough right there.
Not only did he set up Atlantic's international presence, he set Warner Brothers up too. He made them both international companies.

What's the story behind ATCO?
ATCO was the Tonto to Atlantic. Atlantic was successful. They had money and wanted to record more things, so they set up ATCO.

Wasn't ATCO where Atlantic first got into White pop and rock with artists like Sonny & Cher and Dr. John?
Yeah, but it was Bobby Darin's label first. Nesuhi was involved in some of the Darin sessions. He did "Mack the Knife" and "Beyond the Sea." So Nesuhi left, and I got the ball. I stayed until '74, when I left, because I was three inches from bein' thrown out of the building. The kind of jazz that Nesuhi and I produced was over. Fusion was comin' to town, and after that, it was smooth jazz. I didn't do that shit. It was a new Atlantic, and there was no place for me there. Ahmet was signing British groups like Cream, Zeppelin, Emerson, Lake & Palmer, and Yes. He brought the Stones in. So my official welcome was over. By then, Atlantic had become a real company. We had to go to meetings. Once, I had to turn a mix in to the A&R department, and they made some comments. "Well, fuck you, and fuck your comments. That's the way I mixed it!" was all I had to say. [Roberta Flack's] "Killing Me Softly" was turned back. I had to remix it, because the bass drum was too loud. It took [engineer] Gene Paul two weeks to get that fucking sound. So I was in trouble by that time, and Nesuhi was gone most of the time by then.

Didn't you bring [producers] Michael Cuscuna and Hal Willner into the game?
Well, that's the trick. Someone knocks a domino over for you, you knock one over for somebody else. That was all based on my experience with Nesuhi. I learned by instinct.

What defined your style and sensibility as a producer?
I had a left-of-center take. But it was a commercial left-of-center take. I was on point at the time. I knew who to sign and what to do with them. But after '74, what I did in terms of jazz was over. Then I took Rahsaan and Fathead to Warner Brothers, which was semi-disastrous. Rahsaan made some good music with them, but it wasn't great for David. Then I had a hit with Leon Redbone, which sold, like, a million records, so they forgave me my jazz trespasses.

Well, you'd had a huge hit with Les and Eddie's "Compared to What," which was sheer dynamite.
Talk about surrealism, "Compared to What" was the biggest-selling record in the history of Atlantic jazz, and it was the only record that Nesuhi and I produced together, and neither of us were there for the performance! It was Nesuhi's idea to support Claude Nobs and this young jazz festival by sending some Atlantic artists over. He picked Les McCann and Eddie Harris, and in return for Atlantic fronting the expense for the group, Claude gave us back a live audiotape and a videotape from Swiss television. I was the one who told Eddie to sneak up onstage with his reed trumpet and play with Les. And that's when we discovered Guiseppe Pino, one of the greatest photographers in the world, who did so many covers for Atlantic. And then [photographer] Ira Friedlander came in. After Marvin Israel died, we found Stanislaw Zagorski who took care of the graphics. He was unbelievable!

What's your take on free jazz?
I hate that far-out, make-believe jazz/out/downtown shit. It's unlistenable. Everyone we had who was left of center or outside in general, or who could go outside, were all rooted in the tradition. When you heard "Giant Steps," it wasn't Trane just makin' a lot of noise. You knew where he came from, and he changed the rules. When Mingus or Ornette went out, they usually left enough bread crumbs for you to find your way out of the woods. When Yusef or Rahsaan went out, it was cool, you could still hear it. Eddie [Harris], who was the most masterful musician we had until this day, still doesn't get the credit he deserves.

What's the story behind Champion Jack Dupree and King Curtis gettin' together?
So dig this, Curtis and I were over at Montreux. I'm recording guys, and Curtis is playin' with Aretha. Claude Nobs threw a lunch party, and he's got Champion Jack Dupree cookin', makin' a New Orleans meal. After he was done cookin', he sat down at the piano. Curtis finds me and says, "That old man that made lunch, you oughta hear the way he sings." I said, "You fuckin' idiot, that's Champion Jack Dupree." He said, "I never heard him. I wanna make a record with him." I went over to Claude, and I got him a slot the next night and had Jerry Jemmott [on bass] and Al Jackson on drums. I told Nesuhi I wanted to put Curtis's band behind Jack Dupree. He said, "Great, do whatever you want." Not only didn't they rehearse, they had to wait until he played enough of the song to figure out what it was. Then Curtis would come in. It's a great example of something that just happened. Is it the best Jack

Dupree record ever or best King Curtis record ever? No, but it's the best Champion Jack Dupree/King Curtis record ever.

Another great live cut you produced was Rahsaan's "One Ton" from that wild performance he gave at the Newport Jazz Festival.

He was at his lunatic best. We did that at Newport, and George [Wein] wanted him off the stage, but he wouldn't come off. Wein said, "You go get him." I said, "No, you go get him!" Then he threw a gong into the audience. He wouldn't leave the stage. He was crazed. He wanted to steal the festival.

What was the story behind Ray Charles's "Drown in My Own Tears"?

Ray did a concert at a stadium in Atlanta. It was put on by a disc jockey there named Zenas Sears. Since it was done through the auspices of the radio show, they either broadcast it live or taped it and played it at a later date. Ray had left Atlantic for ABC-Paramount when here comes Zenas Sears with the tape made while he was still under contract with Atlantic. Even though Nesuhi made a live album with Ray at Newport, this version of "Drown in My Own Tears" from *Ray Charles in Person* is the single most stunning thing he ever did at Atlantic. You never saw Ray unless you saw him with the small band in the late '50s and very early '60s. When you hear him do "Drown in My Own Tears" like this, you understand what made us crazy—it's the band playing at that tempo and him singin' his ass off and the real Raelettes singin' "Drown in My Own Tears." I'd say there's nothin' in the Atlantic's blues catalog that's better than that.

Tell me about Zawinul's "Soul of a Village, Part 2" from the LP *The Rise and Fall of the Third Stream*.

Joe was still with Cannon[ball Adderley] when I signed him to Atlantic. Cannon got pissed, because I didn't talk to him first. He saw it as a breach and very rude on my part. I didn't realize the protocol. I was, like, twenty-two. It was like when I signed Hubert from Mongo's band. He sent Jack Cook down to beat me up, and we became friends. But I made three records with Joe. A thing called *Money in the Pocket* with Joe Henderson around '65. Zawinul said he had a record he wanted to make with strings, and that's when I met Bill Fischer. [Zawinul] was hot with "Mercy, Mercy, Mercy" at the time, so "Soul of a Village, Part 2" was as close as we could get to that electric piano feel he had. It was jazz, but it was commercial. We had him before Weather Report, and we did a bunch of experimental shit with him. When I was [with] Atlantic, I was trying to make really different jazz records that sold. Nesuhi recorded giants doing their best work at the peak of their talent. Or at the very least, it was some of their best work at a crucial time in their development. Some of it you might think wasn't gonna sell but was valid artistically. I'd try out a lot of stuff with Rahsaan, Yusef, Les, or Eddie.

"Ain't No Sunshine" was just about the most commercial tune that Rahsaan ever cut.

It was one of the few times he agreed to try and make a single. Arif wrote the strings. We were trying to get a single with Rahsaan.

The tone of his flute on that track gives you the chills.

It's an incredible fuckin' record.

As a citizen of the world, Nesuhi was hip to soccer. What was his involvement with the Cosmos?

He signed Pelé! He got him to come to New York and play for the Cosmos. Look, his father was the Turkish ambassador to Switzerland, England, and France. They grew up in embassies all over the world. They were from one of the two or three most prominent families in Turkey. Their father helped get rid of the Ottoman Empire and helped bring Turkey into the twentieth century. Nesuhi was the older brother. There was a five-year difference. He turned Ahmet on to music. When they came to America, they got to hear all the Black artists they loved, jazz and blues guys. He loved New Orleans music but he recorded Ornette, Trane, and Mingus. He made the transition seamlessly. He was very well read in a variety of languages. He knew fourteenth-century Persian poetry as well as twentieth-century authors or French romanticists. He wound up teaching jazz at UCLA. He was the first person to teach a jazz course in the '50s. There were no jazz teachers then! He was a Brahmin, and I was a big-mouth Jew from Philly. I had talent but not a lot of polish. When I was doin' the Midler record, I had real problems. It was the only time Nesuhi couldn't watch my back. Ahmet and Jerry boxed him out. And besides, I was really nuts at that time. You couldn't talk to me. Every record I made sold, and I thought it was because of me. It was partially because of me, but it was because the guys were givin' me some clear highway for a few minutes. I handled success really poorly, and he knew I was nuts, but he still let me go, because what I did was workin'. It was like he had a crazy painter on his hands. He said, "Paint, but stay in your garret, and bring me the paintings, and stay away from everybody." He could have said, "You're really gettin' to be a pain in the ass. Cut it out, or you'll be out of here. So, welcome to my world!" ⬤

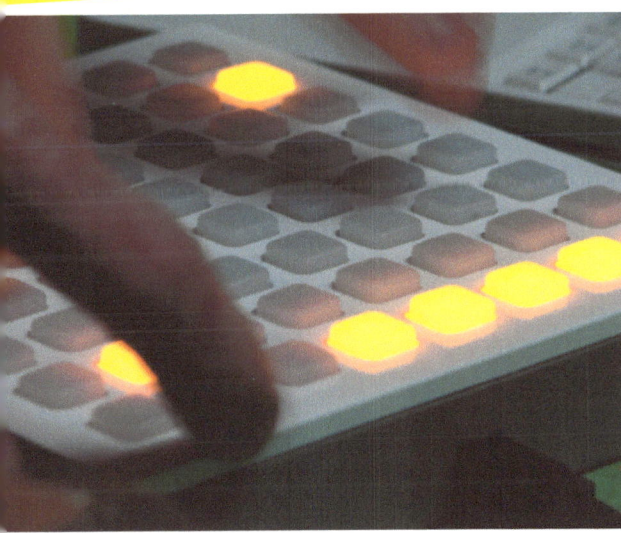

community and online magazine
for bleeding-edge music tech
createdigitalmusic.com

photo by Andrew Lepley/Getty Images

ANALOG OUT
Rhodes Electric Piano

World War II may have given us the atom bomb, but it also contributed what Ray Charles would call "an atom bomb on the musical landscape." Predating synths like the Moog, the Rhodes piano was the great keyboard instrument innovation of the twentieth century. Its history is intertwined with the history of jazz, and while jazz keyboard began on a borrowed European invention, the Rhodes was the first keyboard instrument jazz could call its own.

Harold Rhodes got his start as one of the first jazz theorists and teachers, instructing the likes of Lana Turner and Harpo Marx and hosting his own nationwide instructional radio show. But the basic idea for the Rhodes piano was born when an Army doctor asked Rhodes to soothe bedridden wounded soldiers by teaching them piano. Recycling airplane parts from B-17 bombers into handmade, laptop keyboards, Rhodes first employed the xylophone keys that would later ring inside his signature piano.

After the war, Rhodes worked on mass-manufacturing his pianos, and added the elements that give the Rhodes—and countless jazz records—their sound. The basic innovation was to solve the problem of tuning by turning the entire sound-making mechanism into a tuning fork. As with a conventional piano, the Rhodes has strings struck by hammers. In the Rhodes, these strings are steel wires called "tines," tuned by coil spring. Harold Rhodes added a resonating tone bar behind each string. The combination of the string and bar acts like the two bars of a tuning fork. As with the electric guitar, the electronic amplification of the Rhodes piano gave it the gift of loudness and the timbre-shaping power of effects, changing music forever.

Ironically, it was jazz's great trumpet player Miles Davis who may have had the deepest impact on the instrument. He insisted his musicians adopt the Rhodes and leave behind the history of the acoustic piano. Miles got Herbie Hancock and Chick Corea playing electric piano on his sessions. On the 1969 recording sessions for *Bitches Brew*, as many as three Rhodes pianos blend into new and distorted timbres, helmed by Chick Corea, Larry Young, and "Pharaoh's Dance" composer and Rhodes innovator Joe Zawinul. The same year, the Beatles got an aggressive Rhodes injection from soul musician Billy Preston as they recorded "Get Back." By 1973, the sound of the Rhodes found its way into the pages of *Down Beat* magazine, quite literally, on a four-song demo album by Herbie Hancock included with the magazine. From Stevie Wonder to Radiohead, countless artists have become Rhodes players.

Harold Rhodes died before he could finish his successor to the Rhodes, but he did rescue the trademark from Roland, clearing the way for a new, more modern Rhodes (rhodes-piano.com). Software synth renditions face the challenge of an organic, electro-acoustic instrument. Some use recorded samples (Native Instruments' Elektrik Piano), some physical models (Ableton's Electric); Digidesign's Velvet uses a combination of the two. But perhaps Harold Rhodes's spirit is most alive in the renewed interest in the DIY instrument building he first tried to teach. ○ **Peter Kirn**

Visit waxpoetics.com for more info on Rhodes emulators and to read our interview with the late Harold Rhodes.